DREAM OF ME

DARA GIRARD

ILORI
Press Books, LLC

ISBN: 978-1-949764581

DREAM OF ME

Published by ILORI Press Books

Cover Design and Layout Copyright © 2022 ILORI Press Books

Cover design by ILORI Press Books

Cover Photo © Daxio-Productions/depositphotos

ILORI PRESS BOOKS, LLC

P.O. Box 10332

Silver Spring, MD 20914

www.iloripressbooks.com

Table for Two

Gaining Interest

Careless Rapture

Dangerous Curves

Familiar Stranger

It Happened One Wedding

Unexpected Pleasure

Midnight Promise

Sweet Temptation

Always and Forever

Truly Yours

Say Yes

Picture Perfect

By My Side

Clifton Sisters

The Sapphire Pendant

The Amber Stone

The Emerald Ring

Fortune Brothers

A Tempting Proposal

A Seductive Arrangement

An Unforgettable Moment

Novels

Honest Betrayal

The Daughters of Winston Barnett

Remember My Name

Illusive Flame

Winterwood Lane

Promise Me

This Changes Everything

Sparks

Piece of Cake

Best Laid Plans

Her Tender Touch

CHAPTER ONE

Candice Ayodele knew she was boring.

By nine years old she knew she'd never be the life of the party, the class clown, the smart one or the pretty one. She knew when she shyly smiled at her fourth grade teacher, Mrs. Simmons, at the local farmer's market, one sweet autumn day, and her teacher blinked at her without recognition (even though by that time Candice had been in her class for five months), that she wasn't even a wallflower.

Candice was a wall: Present but easily overlooked or ignored until needed.

Like when someone needed to look at her notes in class or a relative needed a last minute 3AM ride to the airport or a date needed her to pay for dinner because their checking account was overdrawn and they'd forgotten their credit card (they'd treat her next time—funny how there was never a next time). Candice had grown used to people's polite smiles when she attended naming ceremonies or housewarming parties. When she spoke, she'd notice the signs of disinterest as their eyes glazed over or as they surreptitiously searched a ginger scented room for someone else to talk to.

She didn't mind. She started to time the interactions and had an average of five minutes from engagement to escape (their escape not hers). She always felt relieved when the awkward moment ended, when they realized that she wasn't particularly bright, a great conversationalist or well connected.

She preferred to be alone. She marked social gatherings on her calendar with the same enthusiasm as a dentist appointment. Perhaps less so.

She set up her life to avoid as many social interactions as much as possible.

However, in all her thirty years, she'd never been so boring that she'd caused someone to fall asleep.

Her desk chair gently groaned when she leaned back in amazement. She gripped her cell phone, pressing it close to her ear to make sure she wasn't dreaming. She held her breath. In the hushed darkness outside her townhouse, the sound of a truck's tires, driving over the rain soaked street, rose and then fell as it raced past, too fast for their suburban neighborhood; outside her bedroom door, flip flops slapped against the hallway's wooden floor as one of her roommates headed to the kitchen. Then she heard the sound again. A slight catch of breath, not quite a snore but close, that slipped into the sound of a man's soft even breathing on the other end of her phone.

Candice closed her eyes. She heard the white noise of her computer speakers that she'd forgotten to turn off, heat pressing its way through the air vents and...breathing.

His breathing.

His I-find-you-so-astronomically-boring-I-couldn't-stay-awake breathing.

Candice opened her eyes and glanced at the time on her large computer monitor. Granted it was nearly eleven o'clock at night, but really?

She'd waited three months for this moment. Anticipated it. For three months she'd come up with reasons not to exchange phone numbers. To not take their friendship out of the virtual world. But he'd insisted and curiosity had gotten the better of her. She'd caved in spite of her fear that it would end in disaster.

She wasn't even sure how to qualify this. Disaster felt too harsh, embarrassing too tame. It was a strange unsettling, no man's land of humiliation.

She only knew the man on the other end of the phone as V. At first she thought he was referring to himself as the Roman numeral number five until he later clarified that it was just 'vee' but didn't explain farther than that. V was an enigma but his comments, in their forum, were not. They shared their mutual love of the game Flowers of Fortune and Power (FFP). She'd become a devoted player after abandoning another massively multiple player online (MMO) game that suffered numerous delays and almost continually annoying changing features.

Unlike others, FFP wasn't just a dressed up multiple player survival game, it was one of the best story focused MMOs she'd ever played. It wasn't only about getting new gear and leveling up but engaged the player in a complex story world that continued to intrigue her while also setting up beautiful world building and action sequences.

She still didn't remember exactly how they met, whether V sought her out or she'd helped him out, but because she was a high level player she'd seen him get throttled more than once and offered to help him by offering tips and strategies. He proved to be a very quick learner and nimble player and before long they were trading comments and she always looked forward to what he had to say. He always managed to say something intriguing and insightful. They'd soon taken their chats off the main forum into a private one.

She looked forward to late night meetings after work, sometimes in the day (she could set her own hours since she worked from home). She didn't know how old he was. They were careful to keep their offline identities secret. She guessed he was a university student since his hours seemed to fit. But then some of the terms and references he used made him seem a bit older.

The game took her out of her real life. In the real world she was a black woman who worked as a freelance video editor, and sometime web designer, and lived in a townhouse in the surrounding suburbs of a Maryland college town with two roommates who seemed to change every couple years.

At twenty-three she'd bought the townhouse and rented the other rooms to local college students. They all had dreams—the others moved on but Candice's life remained the same. There were graduate degrees achieved, weddings, baby showers then slowly she lost touch or they forgot about her. She didn't dwell on it. Instead she got new roommates and stayed to herself as she usually did, which wasn't hard considering how, at sixteen years old, she'd gotten her video work seen by a small company that eventually contracted her for other projects. She learned that her work spoke for itself so who she was as a person didn't matter much. Text or email was the best mode of communication for her.

As a video editor she made other studios look good. She

could fix other people's work, find what wasn't working or lacking in a scene or frame due to a keen sense of story-telling, pacing and attention to detail. While some of her contemporaries worried about the rise of videographers sending their work to AI services for faster and cheaper rates she didn't care. She had plenty of clients and figured if they started to thin out and the market changed she'd find something else. Rolling with life's ups and downs was what had gotten her through her parent's divorce, her father's remarriage and new family; her mother's second divorce and the death of a cousin who'd been like a brother to her.

Games were her connection to him. Inside game worlds you could be resurrected. You could change, you could live forever. He'd died seven years ago at only twenty-two. Sometimes she wondered how different her life would have been if...

But again she didn't like to dwell on the past.

She really didn't mind being the wall because she had another life.

Another identity.

In the online gaming universe she could be anyone. Anything. She'd been a fire breathing half-cat. A ten year old Victorian girl. A woman who'd returned home to find her family had disappeared. A detective in a dystopian world. Her present avatar in the fantasy, sword bearing world of FFP was Adian, a male warrior of mysterious heritage.

She was a lot more exciting online as Adian. She was confident, never wavering. She collected rewards, gears and defeated enemies easily. People listened when Adian spoke. He was commanding. In control.

V had been a newer player who'd taken to Adian. No surprise, most players did and he was no different, wanting to know how things worked in the world and through a number of battles together they'd enjoyed a camaraderie and soon he became more like a friend.

Friends.

Unlike semi-hermetic Candice, Adian had friends. Lots of them.

But V had broken an unspoken rule: Keep the real world and virtual world separate and she had let him because she'd thought he'd be different.

She'd been wrong again.

CHAPTER TWO

Candice could still remember the sight of the message that had shown up on her screen and frozen her hands, hovering above her keyboard, causing her heart to pound so hard it hurt.

Can we talk?

Not chat. *Talk.* As in offline. As in real time in the real world, with awkward silences and weird pauses and the inability to delete something you hadn't meant to say, talk.

She should have said no. She still didn't know why she hadn't turned him down. But she'd been curious and said *I'm not a guy.* It was a risk to reveal even that much but if it was enough to scare him away she wanted to do it quick.

He didn't respond for a day and she wondered if she'd revealed too much then told herself it didn't matter and went back to playing the game.

He came back later and apologized, said he had a 'work emergency', and then said 'I thought as much' which made her wonder what might have given her away or was he being snarky because he didn't like being tricked. It would be one of the questions she planned to ask him.

They scheduled a time to talk.

She thought about the upcoming phone call all day. She could barely focus on her work. She wondered if she was coming down with a cold because her skin felt clammy, her stomach remained in knots, her head hurt. She thought of canceling and then her cell phone rang.

"Hello Adian."

The sound of V's low, deep voice, like cold water rushing through a dark cave, made her mouth go dry. It felt weird to hear her virtual name spoken. As if her fantasy world had managed to pierce reality somehow. If she'd really been a masculine warrior she would have chosen that voice.

"Hello?" he said again.

Heat crept up her neck then burned her cheeks. She resisted the urge to open a window; to shove her head in a freezer. It was ridiculous that just one word could affect her like this. How would she manage a conversation?

By remembering he knew her as Adian, that's how. She could borrow some of the traits she'd made up for him. Adian was confident, few things fazed him. Certainly not a simple 'hello'.

Candice cleared her throat, straightened in her chair. "Yes, sorry, hello," she said her voice coming out huskier than usual. It got that way when she was nervous, it almost sounded as if she were making fun of his voice. She hoped he didn't think of it that way.

"Thanks for talking to me," he said.

"What did you want to talk about?"

He asked her about the history of the castle at Swerden, a major western realm in FFP. She found that an intriguing question since there were various stories and reasons. The inspiration for the design had several vastly different rumored origins and she thought only two were possible, but she wouldn't dive into that. Instead she'd elaborate on the story world. One criticism of the game was that its initial cutscene was too rushed. The early cinematic, introducing the player to the world, was rushed but the gameplay, the way a player was able to interact and experience the game, made up for it. So she explained the castle's history and expanded on some areas that he may have missed.

She spoke quickly, using simple terms, knowing she could get carried away when she truly enjoyed a topic and Flowers of Fortune and Power was one of her greatest pleasures. She loved sharing it with someone who understood. But she still timed herself. No more than seven minutes. Let him breathe, process, ask questions.

She wouldn't bore him.

But she had.

In spite of all her preparations, the breaks she'd put in her speech pattern, the enthusiasm in her voice, the knowledge she'd shared, she'd bored him to sleep.

At first she didn't know what had happened. She'd laughed at a lame joke another player always said that she repeated and paused to hear V laugh too or groan (that seemed to be the general response) instead she heard nothing.

After a moment of confusion she thought the call had been dropped—disconnected, something!—but she could still hear noises in the background—voices from a movie or a TV show and the meow of a cat, but his breathing had been the biggest clue.

She'd thought of boring a man to tears, but to sleep? This

was definitely a first and did not bode well for any life in the real world.

V had exposed her biggest fear. That she didn't belong in the real world, that she was much better off in a virtual one. She shouldn't have said yes, she should have kept things distant. Now she'd lost a friend. He wouldn't want to know her or Adian after this. The feel of acute loss tightened her throat.

It embarrassed her how much she'd been looking forward to this phone call.

She heard another meow. This time louder as if the cat were directly over the phone.

Candice silently swore.

The wall. V had reminded her that the wall still existed, which was why she always stayed distant from even trying to get close to anyone as much as she wanted to. She looked at the picture of her cousin. They'd taken it together at a beach in Delaware two years before he'd gotten sick. Her cousin had been looking at the camera while Candice had been looking at something off to the side.

His shining eyes and smiling face always proved a comfort to her.

She shook her head at the picture now. "What should I do? Scream in his ear? That would wake him up. No? Too mean? Blast music? What...no it's not the same as screaming, it's jarring but at least I could imagine using Beethoven's 5th. That'd be fun to try. No, okay, you're right. It's late and I wouldn't want to wake anyone else. You're always so considerate. Fine, I'll just hang up and try to forget this ever happened. But I'll never do something like this again."

～

I'M SORRY.

That was the message V sent her the next day.

She didn't reply.

He gifted her a token in the game. An expensive weapon.

She didn't accept it. She eventually would. She wasn't so prideful that she'd turn down a gift like that, but she'd leave it hanging unclaimed and let him sweat a little.

She felt oddly pleased she hadn't lost a friend. He sent another message.

V: *Can I call you?*

Adian: *Why?*

V: *You know why.*

Adian: *I can explain the history of the castle right now. We don't need to talk.*

V: *It's not the same. Please give me another chance.*

She probably shouldn't have, but she did. They selected a different time, an hour earlier.

And he fell asleep again.

They decided to talk about a different subject for their third phone call.

And he fell asleep once more.

It stopped being funny after the fourth time. It hurt.

She stopped accepting his gifts then and blocked his number. He might enjoy having her as his Ambien but she was through. They remained cordial online, but a bond had been broken. He didn't mention it and neither did she.

She made a vow. No contact with people outside of the game.

Unfortunately, it was a vow she wasn't able to keep.

CHAPTER THREE

She knew that voice.

Only by sheer coincidence did Candice end up at the penthouse in downtown Baylor where people spent the equivalent of a monthly mortgage for an average house on pet food.

But she'd been to this zip code plenty of times before, mainly due to her sister's mobile animal grooming business, which seemed to survive any economic times. When times were hard she made her regular amount, when times were booming she made more. Alana was good and could be picky about her clients, but after two rather unfortunate events—one involving a Senator who mistakenly thought Alana could be a bit of 'side fun' and another involving a nanny who became infatuated with Alana and ended up stalking her—her attractive sister made it a rule not to visit certain clients alone.

Unfortunately, Alana's assistant was out sick and she didn't want to cancel an appointment last minute so she asked Candice to join her. Fortunately, Candice had space between projects so her schedule was free.

Candice always proved a good deterrent. At 5'10 with what many would call 'androgynous' features, veering more on the side of handsome than pretty, and shoulder length twists pulled back in a ponytail, at first glance people thought she was a guy. Compared to Alana's slender, softer features and bob cut, sleek black hair the contrast was even more striking and the sisters used it to their advantage.

Their family had expected a rivalry between them. Alana was everything Candice wasn't. But Alana instantly loved her baby sister—there was a three year age gap—and although Alana quickly learned Candice didn't like dressing up in frilly play clothes or having tea time, she quickly changed their games and Alana played the lady of the manor and Candice the butler or Alana owned a fashion boutique and Candice ran the outdoor gear store next door. They supported each other and accepted each other. Alana even accepted that Candice didn't really have any female friends outside of her and although she tried, unsuccessfully, to introduce her to others, had given up. Alana had girlfriends she went shopping with, spent girls' night with, to go on beach vacations and Candice was happy for her.

On the other hand, Candice enjoyed what she considered a secret power. Around seven years old she learned that with the right disguise, which took minimal effort (a baseball cap, a pair of glasses) she could pass for a boy. While in disguise she got to play a local game of soccer with the boys and walk into the boy's section of the clothing store without hassle. As an adult, she learned it was a great way to protect her sister. So their time together was usually spent like this:

Candice being a semi-bodyguard in the shadow of her sister's light.

"I'm a little scared of this one," Alana had told her as they rode the elevator.

"Why?"

"There's something about him that gives me the sense he might be a problem."

"What breed?"

Her sister blinked. "Breed?"

"The cat. You're grooming a cat, right?"

Alana laughed. "I wasn't talking about the cat. I was talking about the man. You should know me by now. Animals rarely intimidate me. It's their owners who usually cause the most trouble."

"True. So who is this guy? Should I put my sunglasses on? I can look extra fierce if you want me to."

"No, it'll be fine. He's the CEO of some consulting company."

"Which narrows it down considerably," Candice said in a sarcastic tone.

"Sorry, I didn't pay attention. He came to me through a referral. That's the only thing that matters to me and he checks out."

"But you're nervous."

"I hope he's not hard to manage. He sounded massive and intimidating on the phone."

"I'm sure it will be fine."

But the moment Jarell Ventura opened the front door Candice wasn't so sure. He was one of the few men who could make her feel small. Although she guessed him to only be a couple inches above her height, he seemed much taller. Bigger. Her eyes shifted from a large hand holding the door open, to his large stocking feet. A blue Henley shirt stretched across a broad chest, and jeans clung to well-formed thighs. She'd never paid attention to a man's thighs before. But this man—this cocoa colored man with eyes that didn't seem quite focused, as if his mind were elsewhere or he was just bored—caught her attention.

But then he spoke and her heart stopped.

He said 'hello'. One word. But one word was all it took to get her mind racing, leaving her slightly breathless. She *knew* that 'hello'. She'd heard that 'hello' before. The first time she'd heard that 'hello' she thought she'd burst into flames. But no. That was impossible. It had to be. He couldn't be V. No. No way. He was a big man with a deep voice. Plenty of men had deep voices that reminded her of dark caves or smooth chocolate melting over hazelnuts. This voice was not out of the ordinary. A voice like that for a man of his size was to be expected. Her imagination was getting the best of her.

"Do you need help with any of your equipment?"

Alana looked at him for a moment tongue-tied and Candice couldn't blame her. Aside from his looks it was rare that a client was so cordial. Usually she dealt with other service staff or a hovering owner who would pass by her as she carried tons of equipment. Candice watched her sister quickly recover herself and offer him a bright smile. "No, thanks. We're fine. Just show us a well lit area with plenty of outlets where you want us to set up."

"There's plenty of space in the living room," he said, closing the door behind them, and she became aware of the scent of baked plantain and a hint of curry. "Move things around if you need to. I also have the two dry towels and trash bags you requested."

That voice. Why was that voice coming from this man?

That voice had imprinted itself in her auditory memory. On the phone, that voice that had felt intimately close.

"Candice?"

She blinked and stared at her sister who was looking at her in a weird way. Jarell was too except his gaze wasn't curious, it was intense. Laser focused. It was then that Candice realized she hadn't moved and they were several yards ahead of her. She grabbed her bags and followed.

No, she had to be mistaken. It couldn't be true.

It couldn't be...

Her mind faded to black when she saw his living room. She knew this man. In a way she *was* this man. The elegant minimal décor, the selected color choice—black, dark green, silver—was from the Eldenmere Realm of the game. She and V had discussed them before. Her eyes fell on two pillows on his black couch. Then she saw it... The symbol on a pillow only other gamers would know. To an unknown eye it looked like a sleek decorative piece, but to a trained eye, like hers, she knew it was the flower of death and resurrection. One that changed colors depending on the season.

The décor was so subtle but anyone with a keen eye could recognize another member of the tribe. She wondered why he'd chosen that particular flower.

She gripped her hand into a fist. No, she couldn't wonder that. She couldn't wonder anything. But she did. She wondered why there was so much black, certain elements could have been brightened with tomato red throw pillows, complimented with a warmer grey accent instead of such a cool silver, but they'd be minor changes. This place was wonderful. She felt as if she knew him, as if he'd know her. Then her eyes fell on something that wiped away any doubt. In the corner she saw his gaming station. An untrained eye would see an office desk, perhaps a futuristic looking high back office chair, but she knew better. The sleek design, the two 27" monitors and the mechanical keyboard with detachable cushioned wrist rest (she owned the exact same model) it was perfect for MMOs.

"What's wrong?"

She looked at her sister then saw Jarell studying her. His eyes no longer seeming as unfocused as before. They met hers. Held hers. Not with intimidation but narrowing with a slight silent question: What do you *really* see?

She saw too much. That was usually her problem. Only moments before he'd been a big but somewhat bored looking man, but now she had to wretch herself from his mesmerizing dark brown eyes and try not to notice the velvet soft darkness of his lashes and brows.

She needed to leave. But she couldn't leave her sister alone.

Alana didn't know about her secret life as a gamer, she couldn't tell her about this man. She opened her mouth then realized two awful things. One she couldn't explain anything about her strange behavior with him standing there, two she couldn't speak *at all* because if she did he might recognize her voice.

If only she didn't have such a distinctive voice. At ten she'd been teased that she sounded like a drag queen. At sixteen they'd compared her to a phone sex operator who'd smoked too many cigars.

Maybe Jarell wouldn't put the two together, but she couldn't risk it.

His sharp gaze could have frozen her words anyway.

"Are you all right?" he asked her. "Do you need to sit down?"

Candice considered putting on an accent. She was pretty good with those. She'd been told she was pretty good with Southern (she'd had a great aunt, she'd adored, on her mother's side who'd hailed from Georgia), Hindu (she'd watched enough Bollywood movies with her paternal grand-mother to sing songs in perfect harmony) or Irish accent (just because she could mimic the cadence). Of course she was spot on with her West African accent (specifically southern Nigerian and posh) due to her father and various relatives, but then her sister would look at her strange. That wouldn't work. She'd have to feign illness.

"I'm coming down with—," She was about to say 'a cold' but then she didn't want him to think she was contagious, "laryngitis," she said in a hoarse voice.

Such a hoarse dry voice, it tickled the back of her throat and she began to cough. "Excuse me," she wheezed before she hurried out of the room.

"Are you sure she's all right?" she heard him say, which was very annoyingly considerate of him. She couldn't ruin this for her sister. This job was to be a simple bath, blow-dry, brush out and nail trim. She would follow orders as usual, nod when appropriate and then it would be over.

CHAPTER FOUR

"*L*aryngitis?"

Jarell had gone to another room and had left Candice and Alana alone with his cat Alfonso: A large muscular cat that seemed to mimic his owner in cat form, except that he had long white and grey hair and one eye. He sat very docile and patient on the portable table which made the job easy, but not comfortable.

"I know he looks terrifying," Alana continued, while trimming Alfonso's nails. "But I didn't expect you to freeze like that."

Candice looked around to make sure he was no way within hearing distance before she whispered, "I'll explain later."

Alana put the nail trimmer away and brushed him again. "He is gorgeous though. Almost obscenely so. And doesn't he know it."

She thought her sister was being overly generous, Jarell had a nice face but he was far from swoon worthy. "I don't think he's gorgeous. He looked kind of tired to me."

Alana lifted up Alfonso's face and peered closer. "Tired? He doesn't look tired to me."

Candice inwardly groaned. The cat. Of course her sister was talking about the cat.

"Never mind."

"Is he behaving himself?" Jarell said, coming up behind her.

Alana stroked the cat unaware her sister had turned to stone. "He's a doll."

Jarell moved to the head of the table so he could face them both. "No hissing? No spitting?"

"I know you warned me about that," Alana said with a laugh, "but he's been a perfect gentleman. He even licked Candice's hand."

Yes, that had surprised her too. But she didn't appreciate her sister directing Jarell's attention to her when it was the last thing she wanted.

"Really?" Jarell said, drawing out the word, his eyes narrowing a fraction as he studied Candice with renewed interest. "I'm surprised. He's not usually this calm with strangers."

Candice just shrugged and smiled in response, hoping he got the message. *It's no big deal. Don't think of it as a big deal. Don't think about it at all.*

"You must have a special touch."

She quickly shook her head and motioned to her sister. *Please look at her! Please ignore me. Please pretend I'm not here. Most people do.* She wanted him to see the magic Alana had done with Alfonso. How sleek, shiny and healthy his fur looked. But Jarell didn't look to where she'd gestured. Instead, he'd folded his arms and took a step towards her and opened his mouth as if he was going to ask a question.

Fortunately, Candice's cell phone rang, cutting off his words. She inwardly swore. People knew better than to call her. If they called it was usually because they were panicked about something. She pulled out her phone and glanced at the number and sure enough it was a client who was known for his epic meltdowns. She flashed Jarell an apologetic grin then motioned towards his kitchen, asking if she could answer it in there. His eyes narrowed a little more and she wondered what he was thinking, but then he nodded and she raced out of the room.

It took her ten minutes to calm down the panicky client. She was good in a crisis; she didn't get overexcited and tended to make people trust her. "It's going to come within budget. Yes, it's taking a little longer but that was expected as I explained to you earlier. No, I'm not using that raw footage because as I said it's too grainy and will upset the rest of the film's balance. Yes, you can take this project elsewhere. As our agreement states you are within the window to do that. Of course I understand you're stressed, but I need you to trust me. Okay? Good. Yes, I'll get back to you next week. You'll be pleased. Yes, yes I know. You're welcome. Bye."

She disconnected. One minor disaster averted. Alana should soon be finished with Alfonso and she could avert another.

Candice heard movement behind her, she felt her skin prickle. There was someone in the kitchen with her. Please let it be Alana. Or the cat. Please let it be the cat that smells like men's cologne.

She slowly turned and saw exactly what she'd dreaded. Jarell stood there, leaning against the corner of the wall with a smug smile on his face.

He'd heard her speaking. Or maybe he hadn't. Or

perhaps if he had, he'd just think she was weird for making up a silly lie but not think anything of it.

Please don't let him have heard me.

Jarell folded his arms. "Hello, Adian."

CHAPTER FIVE

*D*igging a hole in the ground and jumping into it was not an option. Unlike in Flowers of Fortune and Power, she couldn't sign off and disappear. She had to stand there and think.

She could feign innocence. "What? Adian who?"

Jarell lifted a knowing brow.

Innocence wouldn't work.

She could feign surprise. She grabbed her throat. "Amazing how laryngitis can just clear up."

He blinked.

That wouldn't work either.

Ignore him. She made a move to walk past him. "I need to—"

"I wondered why a person with laryngitis would be answering calls instead of texting. Now I know." His hands fell to his hips. "Why did you lie?"

"I didn't lie."

He grabbed his throat. "I have laryngitis," he said in a dramatically hoarse voice.

He was right. She did lie. And it wasn't a tiny lie. It was a big flaming lie. But she didn't want to explain it. She walked past him. "I need to help Alana clean up and then—"

"Adian," he called after her.

Candice spun around and glared at him. "Stop calling me that."

"This doesn't have to be awkward."

"Of course it's awkward. Not only did I never picture meeting you in real life, I'm afraid to talk to you."

"Why?"

She leaned her head back and mimed someone fast asleep and snoring. She lifted her head and folded her arms. "Bring back any memories?"

He leaned against the counter, a flash of embarrassment crossing his face. "A little."

"Every time I talk to you, I make you fall asleep." She pointed at him. "Even now your eyes are slowly closing and your arms are becoming slack."

Jarell shook his head as if to rouse himself and ran a hand down his face with chagrin. "Sorry, bad night."

"I don't care, I'm going to fake laryngitis until I'm out of here." She mimed zipping her lips shut.

He hesitated. "I need a favor."

She shook her head.

"Please."

She shook her head with more force and waved her hands.

"Does your sister know you play a 6'7 foot male in a virtual game?"

She mimed unzipping her lips. "Are you blackmailing me?"

"I'm desperate."

"I'll take that as a yes."

He pressed his hands together. "Please. I wouldn't ask otherwise."

She glanced away. She should say no. Saying yes to this guy always ended up disappointing her.

He got down on his knees. "Please."

"Get up."

He prostrated himself. "I'm begging you," he said, his voice muffled by the ground.

She rushed over to him and tried to lift him up. "Stop that!" She tried to raise his arm but it was impossible to move him. She'd have more success trying to shift a volcano.

He rolled onto his back and looked up at her. "I told you I'm desperate." He closed his eyes.

Watching his velvet soft lashes shadowed on his cheeks transported her to the game. The sight reminded her of when he'd been defeated by one of the gargoyles. Of course he hadn't looked like this. The V she knew wore an eye patch, was shorter and leaner with spiked purple hair (her avatar was a man so she wouldn't judge). She'd knelt by his body just like this as a gentle rain fell. She'd come too late to rescue him and had made a promise then that she'd help him to get stronger.

But this wasn't some grassy landscape with an orchestral soundtrack in the background, this was a penthouse kitchen where she heard the sound of ice shifting in the refrigerator's ice maker and she could feel the lingering heat of the cooling stove, but he still looked half dead. His mouth tight, his jaw tense. If he was truly desperate there was no harm in hearing him out even if she'd eventually say no. He needed hope.

She sighed in defeat, resting a hand on his shoulder. "Fine, what is it?"

He opened his eyes and jumped to his feet with an agility that surprised her. She stared up at him, absently taking his hand when he extended it out to her. He lifted her to her feet with careless ease before he glanced at his watch, looked over his shoulder, as if he feared they'd be overheard, then he lowered his voice and said, "There's a coffee shop next door."

"The one that charges you the price of a new kidney for a medium latte?"

"It's not that expensive." Before she could argue he held up his hand. "I'll pay. Just meet me there at three o'clock tomorrow and I'll tell you what I need you to do."

"What happened in there?" Alana demanded on the elevator ride down to the parking garage. "I know you're usually bad with people but this was on the verge of a melt-down. You were so terrified of him that you had to fake having laryngitis?"

Candice shifted the bag on her shoulder and watched the elevator numbers descend. "I wasn't terrified of him."

"You looked terrified. Twice he asked me if he'd done or said anything to spook you."

Candice turned to her. "And what did you tell him?"

"I told him my sister was crazy and to just ignore her."

"Ha ha."

"Really. What happened?"

She returned her gaze to the red digital numbers. "He... reminded me of someone. I'm sorry, I can't explain it more than that. "

"You nearly ruined this job for me."

Candice swallowed, feeling her throat tighten. "I know. I'm sorry."

Alana paused before she said, "Have you ever considered seeing someone about—"

Candice shifted the bag to her other shoulder. "I said I was sorry, okay? It's never happened before and it won't again so let's drop it. I'm fine."

"You're not fine. You haven't been fine since—"

"I will never be outgoing and bubbly like you."

"No one is asking you to be. But you barely leave your house except when you're forced to for the holidays, family gatherings or I ask you to help me. You're isolated. I think you should get out more. Date."

Candice rolled her eyes and lightened her voice to an exaggeratedly girlish tone. "Of course, because finding a man will solve *all* my problems."

Alana frowned. "That's not what I mean."

"Perhaps I'll just find some random guy and sleep with him, pass him off as my boyfriend for a while so that I can be deemed normal. Thanks for that advice."

Alana released a long sigh. "You scared me today."

"What?"

"The way you responded to Jarell wasn't normal."

"Jarell?"

"Yes, that's his name."

She knew that but it felt strange hearing her sister use it. It forced her to see him clearly in the real world. Jarell Ventura. Something clicked. Now she knew what V stood for. The first letter in his last name. That was one mystery solved. Sigh, the man had no imagination.

"It was like you'd seen a ghost or something. It was

strange. You were terrified but also strangely happy as if you'd found something you'd been searching for."

The elevator stopped and the doors opened. Candice stepped out, relieved to escape the metal box. "Why are you making up stories?"

"I'm serious," Alana said following her. "I think Jarell noticed it too. He kept looking at you in an intense way."

Candice gripped the strap of her bag, annoyed by the ease in which her sister used his name. As if she knew him. Making new connections always came so easy to her. Given a couple more minutes, Alana could get him to reveal his past, make him laugh and secure a two year retainer agreement. Candice wasn't sure she could use his real name yet. She could repeat his name in her mind, but not get it past her lips. The only thing she could get him to do in real life was fall asleep. "Guys like him always look at things in an intense way."

"Tell me what happened."

She couldn't. She heard a car coming and stopped to let her sister walk ahead of her. She felt a slight breeze as a black Porsche whizzed past them.

"Candice?"

She couldn't tell her the truth but she could tell her something close. "He reminded me a little bit of...our cousin." Her tongue felt heavy in her mouth. She knew she didn't need to specify which one. "I-I thought if he'd lived his place would have looked like that."

Alana released a heavy sigh. Her voice trembled a bit when she spoke, "You're right. He would have loved that place."

"And Alfonso?"

"I think he would have stolen him." He'd had a weakness for disfigured animals.

They laughed at the thought then fell into silence.

"I know you miss him," Alana said in a quiet voice when they finally reached her light copper colored SUV, which looked liked the unfortunate love child of a minivan and a penny.

"Don't—"

She opened the trunk. "But you can't live in the past."

"I'm not."

"You're living with roommates you don't like."

"I don't mind them."

"Stuck with clients you don't like."

"Only a few get on my nerves."

"And haven't gone on a hike in years. You used to love those. We would all..."

"Yeah," Candice cut in not wanting to reminisce, not wanting to fully feel the sting of her sister's criticism. "I've been busy. But someday."

"Right, someday," Alana said unconvinced.

"I will." Candice said, knowing her sister had a right to feel that way. She knew she kept pushing off 'someday'. It sounded like a lie even to her own ears. But what was the point of a hike that only filled her with painful memories?

"So what did you two talk about in the kitchen?" When she turned to her sister surprised, she grinned. "I may not have gotten the words but your voice carries."

"It was nothing. " Candice put her large bag in the trunk. "He caught me talking on my cell phone and I had to explain why I lied."

"You must have given him a good reason because he gave me a generous tip."

"I'm glad I didn't ruin the job for you."

"Actually, to be honest, I lied too. You didn't nearly ruin it. I think you were my lucky charm. Both he and Alfonso seemed to like you."

Candice forced a smile. Jarell hadn't liked her. He just saw her as a useful wall he could lean on.

CHAPTER SIX

andice didn't arrive at the café at precisely three o'clock because Jarell had blackmailed her. She didn't care if her sister found out about her avatar (her roommates on the other hand would have been a nightmare, but he hadn't threatened to tell them). She arrived at precisely three o'clock because she was curious.

However after twenty minutes of waiting, her curiosity turned to anger. She stood to leave when Jarell barged through the front door with enough force that heads turned, looking the image of a disheveled businessman—loose tie, one side of his shirt hanging out—before collapsing in the seat in front of her. She half expected the earth to shake from the impact of his large body colliding with the wooden seat. "Sorry," he said.

"And the bad manners just keep coming," Candice said oddly pleased to see him again, relieved that he hadn't stood her up.

He tucked in his shirt and tightened his tie. "I sent you a text that I'd be running late."

"You did not send me a text."

He smoothed down the tie. "I was sure I did."

His tie still looked bad, the loop was too fat and it was crooked. Candice told herself she didn't care (although her fingers were itching to fix and straighten it). She looked at her cell phone and scrolled through her messages. "Nope. Nothing. Unless it was an imaginary one."

Jarell frowned. "I was sure I sent it." He scratched his chin. "I thought about it... I thought about you sitting here..." He swore as a realization struck him. His hand fell to the table. "But I must not have followed through."

"A habit of yours?"

"I'm sorry."

"Sending a text can be so taxing," she said in a voice heavy with sarcasm. "My thumbs ache just at the thought of it."

He sighed. "Truly sorry."

She put her cell phone away. "Yes, we've established that." She pushed over a thermos. "It's still warm."

"What is it?"

She sent him a look, surprised he even had to ask. "Coffee. Deep roast."

"You ordered for me?"

She couldn't tell by his tone whether he was annoyed or pleased, but she did notice his gaze sharpen in a way that made her cheeks warm.

She looked at his mouth. Nope, bad move. She shifted her gaze to his shirt, but then she fixated on his damn tie and that was annoying. She glanced toward the counter. "It wasn't hard, you seem to be a regular here. I described you to the barista and she made this." She nodded to the thermos.

"How did you describe me?"

"As an enormous black man with sleepy eyes."

He rested his chin in his hand. "No, you didn't."

"It's a silly question."

He shrugged. "I was just curious."

"How would you describe me?"

He looked at her for a long moment then said, "You're right, it's a silly question."

"But I still answered it."

"You didn't answer it truthfully."

"How do you know?"

"Because I know you."

"You do not know me."

He lifted a sly brow. "I know you enough that you didn't describe me like that."

He was challenging her to argue with him. The slight lift of his eyebrow was a dangerous signal. He was not one to be underestimated, despite his shabby appearance. The raised eyebrow made him look devious. V could be devious too. But he wasn't V right now. He was Jarell and he wanted a favor.

"The thermos is mine," she said, "so I'll want it back, but I didn't know when you'd come and I wanted your coffee to stay hot."

He glanced at his palm before he removed the thermos top, poured coffee into it and took a sip then nodded impressed. "Thanks." He studied the thermos before he set it back down. "I'll buy you a new one."

"Why would you buy me a new one?"

He took another sip. "Because I'm keeping this one. I'm impressed and few things impress me."

"But you can order—"

He took a long swallow, his gaze meeting hers over the steaming rim. He spoke in a low voice. "I want this one."

Since the thermos held no sentimental value she wouldn't argue with him. She'd bought it for a hiking trip that had never happened. "Okay."

He set the cup down. "No coffee for you?"

"I finished my coffee twenty minutes ago. I also had a muffin."

"I said I'd pay. What do I owe you?"

"Your first born."

The corner of his mouth kicked up in a quick grin. "Already spoken for." He turned to the counter and looked at the choices on the board. "Tell me what you had."

"A pistachio Danish and iced coffee."

Jarell turned sharply to her. "That isn't coffee."

Candice folded her arms. "Are you judging my beverage choice?"

"Absolutely. Milk, ice and syrup isn't coffee."

"It had some espresso."

"Enough to fill a thimble half way."

She grinned. "And it was delicious."

He shook his head disappointed. "You might as well have tea."

"They don't have my favorite herbal blend."

He visibly shivered, but fought to keep his expression neutral. "You like...herbal?"

She laughed. "Not really, but I had to see how much of a beverage snob you are."

"I'm not a snob. I was just brought up to have good taste."

"We'll agree to disagree." She rested her arms on the

table. "So, you've got your boringly traditional hot coffee. That should keep you awake for at least fifteen minutes. Better start talking."

He bit his lip and looked chagrined. "About that." He took a deep breath. "I'm sorry."

"You've said that more than once. Perhaps if you said it in another language it would have more meaning."

He bowed and said 'I'm sorry' in Japanese. Then pressed his hands together and said the words in Portuguese before he bowed again and said the words in Yoruba.

Candice shook her head. "Okay, that was just weird."

"Not impressive?"

The Portuguese hadn't surprised her. With a name like Ventura it made sense. The Yoruba was a shock, but then he could have been Brazilian Nigerian. Now the Japanese...that was surprising and almost pitch perfect but she didn't want to admit it. She found him funny and surprising and likeable. But that didn't matter. She wanted to hear what he had to say and then leave. "What do you want?"

He poured another cup, took a long sip, sighed, tugged on his tie—making it worse. "You have this affect on me."

"Yes, I'm so boring I put you to sleep."

He leaned forward and lowered his voice. "I haven't been able to sleep well for more than a year. But the past six months have been the worst. It's one of the reasons I joined the game, I needed something to do. Reading a boring book and streaming a video wasn't working. Flowers of Fortune and Power kept me sane. And then...the first night I spoke to you...I didn't even realize I was falling asleep until the next morning and I'd never had such a good night's rest in months."

She didn't know whether to feel happy or insulted.

"It was the same the other times too. You calm me."

Candice folded her arms. "So you want me to call you every night so you can fall asleep?"

"I need more than that. I need you to go away with me for a long weekend."

CHAPTER SEVEN

Her arms fell to her sides. "What?"

"In three weeks I've got an important business meeting with a venture capitalist and I want to be at my best. Lately I've been making mistakes, forgetting things, and I can't afford that. Like now, when I thought I'd texted you and I didn't. I can't do that there."

"I can just call you—"

He turned his palm to face him and glanced at it. "It's a cabin in the Adirondack Mountains with no reception. The person I'm meeting with is a little eccentric and thinks a wireless retreat in the wilderness will reveal a person's character and focus their mind. He's known for not really caring about ideas and business strategies. He only invests in people he likes so I have to be at my best. I promise I'll make it worth your time. It will only be three nights."

"Have you tried medicine?"

"I've tried medicine, hypnosis, acupuncture, therapy. Nothing seems to work except..."

He let the words trail off, leaving her to fill in the rest. He looked at her with tired, pleading eyes.

Sad, lovely brown eyes.

Warm chocolate brown eyes.

No. No. No, she didn't want to.

"If you've functioned this long what difference would three nights be?" she said. "I haven't put you to sleep in a while and you seem to be okay."

"I can manage for short segments," he said through clenched teeth. "But I'm pushing it. This is my tenth cup of coffee today. Not to mention two energy drinks."

"That's insane."

"I know."

"And could be dangerous."

"I'm running on empty and I don't know what else to do."

The desperation wasn't just on his face but in his voice too. Candice felt her resolve weakening. What would three nights of talking him to sleep hurt? He needed help.

"If I go with you, promise you'll seek therapy again."

His eyes brightened with hope. "So you'll do it?"

"You haven't promised me."

He sighed. "I told you—"

"Promise."

He shook his head. "It won't make a difference."

"Go to a different therapist."

"Fine. I promise."

"Good."

He smiled with such relief that it highlighted the shadows under his eyes and made her realize how tense his expression had been. "You really haven't slept this week?"

He tugged on his tie. "I think I've gotten four hours."

"A night?"

"This entire week."

That sounded awful. She leaned closer and lowered her voice. "You said this started about a year ago? But got really bad six months ago? Do you know what triggered it?"

He lifted his coffee and took a sip.

He either didn't know the answer or didn't plan to tell her. Fair enough, it was dangerous to be too curious about him. They weren't friends. They weren't V and Adian fighting battles together and chatting in the local tavern. He wanted a favor and then she'd likely never hear from him again both offline and on. She felt as if she'd lost something but didn't want to dwell on it.

She sat back. "I could just record my voice."

"Tried that, didn't work."

"Oh, well then...wait. You recorded my voice?"

His gaze shifted to the side. "It wasn't on purpose.'"

"I don't believe you."

He met her eyes. "Want to press charges?"

"Is that a challenge?"

He held up a hand. "I told you I've been making mistakes. I don't even know what I was trying to do when it happened. But the next thing I knew I had your voice recorded on my phone and I decided to test it out."

She folded her arms on the table. "I won't help you if you won't be truthful with me."

"Okay, you're right. I did it on purpose. It was only for a couple minutes. After I fell asleep the first time I...I wanted to hear what you'd said. It wasn't my finest hour. I liked your back story about the castle by the way."

She couldn't believe he'd tried to go to sleep using a recording of her voice.

"I don't know what it is about you talking in real time. Please. As I said—"

"Fine, I'll do it. What's the plan?"

He released a long sigh, glanced at his palm. "I could also—"

She waved her hands in front of his face. "Earth to Jarell, I just said yes."

He looked up from his hand. "You did?"

"Yes. Give me your hand." She shook her head when he held out his right hand. "No, the other one."

He drummed his fingers. "Why do you want to see it?"

"Why don't you want to show me?"

He sighed then held out his hand where he'd scribbled on his palm. His hand was just as big as she'd remembered it to be. But she didn't remember it being so nice to look at. He had long, strong fingers, beautiful deep lines crossing his palm. She didn't know anything about palm reading but his looked like it would be fun to figure out. However, what surprised her was that they weren't handwritten notes but pictures. She spotted a cup. What looked like a house. A square with a dollar sign in the middle. She looked through one image that seemed to have been smudged but looked like a flower and a star. "What is this?"

He pulled his hand away. "I was prepared to have to convince you more."

"You don't have much confidence in your skills of persuasion."

"That's not it."

"What is it then?"

He opened his mouth, bit his lip, then took another sip of the coffee before he clasped his hands together, leaving another question to go unanswered. She was starting to regret giving up her thermos so freely. "I'll want to sleep by eleven the latest," he said.

"Okay."

"And I'll need you in my room."

"Fine. I'll sit by your bed and read you something..." She fell silent when he shook his head. "What?"

"That won't work," he said.

"What won't work?"

He sipped his coffee then set it down. "Reading to me."

"How do you know that won't work?"

"I just do. It's when you talk that—"

Candice rolled her eyes trying to make light of a painful reality. "I bore you into oblivion, I get it."

His face grew serious. "It's not that. I just—"

"You shouldn't dismiss something you haven't even tried."

"I know it won't work."

"Perhaps we should do a trial run," she said, starting to doubt his plan and his sense. He hadn't slept well in awhile and it was clearly affecting his thinking. "We need to make sure this is the right strategy. What if you take me all the way to some cabin in New York and this plan doesn't work? We'd be wasting both our time."

"My plan will work, but," he nodded as if coming to a decision, "a trial run sounds like a good idea."

"Don't sound so surprised, I've saved your life more than once, remember?" she said referring to the game.

The hint of a smile touched his lips. He took another sip then said in a soft, knowing voice. "I remember."

She didn't know whether it was the words or how he said them but suddenly the air between them sizzled with a new intimacy. As if they were no longer in a coffee shop, but somewhere with only the two of them and he was seeing something deep within her she didn't want him to see. She cleared her throat. "So we should try a test first. Do you nap?"

"Schedule's too busy for naps."

"But—"

"Besides I'm not testing this theory on a nap. It'd feel like a waste."

"Naps are a great way to recharge. Just ask the unfortunately named Alfonso."

Jarell's brows shot up. "You don't like my cat's name?"

"I don't think he likes it either. How long have you had him?"

"Not long." He paused. "What would you call him?"

"Sika. It means—"

"I'm not giving my cat a Zulu name."

"Why not?"

"Try again."

"Oru."

He nodded, thoughtful. "Night. Yes, that will work. It'll be his nickname."

"You're keeping the name Alfonso?"

"Yes, and no, I'm not explaining why." He yawned.

She realized her time was running out. The last thing she needed was for him to fall asleep at the table. "We're getting off the subject. Let's focus on our experiment."

His eyes grew a little hazy and he slowly licked his bottom lip. "Experience?"

"Experiment. What is wrong with you?"

He blinked. Rubbed his eyes. Shook his head. "Sorry."

"Obviously the coffee is wearing off so I'll talk fast. Are

you busy tomorrow night? No? Good. I'll come by before eleven. Say ten forty-five. I'll bring a really boring book."

"Make sure it has nothing to do with the history of robotics and causal correlation."

She frowned. "That's strangely specific."

"I know."

"I've never even heard of it, but what do you have against it?"

"Nothing. That's the problem. My girlfriend thought reading that to me would help, but I found it interesting instead."

"You're not kidding?"

"No."

"Wait," Candice said as his words settled into her mind. "You have a *girlfriend?* Did you tell her about this idea? How will you explain—"

Jarell rubbed his face again. "Sorry, I meant ex-girlfriend." He yawned. "We broke up a few months ago."

"I'm sorry."

He flashed a sleepy smile. "You should be," he mumbled, but before she could ask 'why' he said, "It's okay."

"Was it the game? Did you break up because of that?"

He slowly blinked and shook his head. "No."

She wasn't going to ask him what he meant by that. She was quickly losing him. "Okay, so I'll come by tomorrow night—"

He rested his chin in his hand, his eyes heavy. "Why not tonight?"

"Don't you think it's too soon?"

"I'm leaving for New York in three weeks. That will come sooner than we expect. I don't think we should wait too long."

"True, you're about to face plant into the table."

He stretched out his arms. "Sorry, it's really not you."

"It is me. That's why you asked me here and why I'll see you later tonight. Lean forward."

He did and she pulled off his tie. She wrapped it around her neck and tied it before putting it back over his head and fastening it around his neck. She sat back pleased. "Much better."

An affectionate grin softened his face. "Thanks."

"I'll find a book that will have you asleep in no time," Candice said then abruptly stood, aware she was in danger of not only being affected by his smile but the light hint of mischief in his eyes.

CHAPTER EIGHT

It wasn't too late to change her mind.

Candice stood outside Jarell's apartment door. She'd twice raised her hand to knock before letting her hand fall. She should cancel. What if this didn't work? What if it did?

She gasped when the door swung open.

"How long are you planning on standing there?" Jarell asked her. Or rather growled, he looked tired and tense.

She adjusted her large canvas bag. "I don't know."

He pulled her inside with such force she briefly collided with his bare chest, briefly encased in the sweet smell of tangerines, before taking a hasty step back. She looked down then swiftly lifted her gaze again, but it didn't help. Her heart continued to pound. There was just too much of him to see.

He wasn't completely naked, but...close. She couldn't look at him so she'd look at his place instead.

"How did you know I was outside?" she asked him.

"I've got cameras."

"Oh." Of course he did.

She heard the door close.

His place felt different at night.

She didn't know if it was from the warm glow of the lamplights, the scent of tangerines, but the darkness of his décor felt even more prominent in the evening. Intense. Absorbing. The apartment was still stylistically elegant but a little unsettling as well. Plus she was alone with him and she hadn't been alone with him before. Without her sister's bubbly presence she felt unmoored in a dark sea. And it didn't help that he was...

Candice took a deep breath. There was nothing to worry about. She wouldn't be there long. Probably fifteen minutes then he'd be out like a light. She had to be as casual as he was.

She swung her arms and feigned a light tone. "Well, I guess I'm lucky you don't go to bed naked."

Jarell frowned. "What do you mean?"

"I thought you'd at least wear pajama bottoms."

He rested his hands on his hips, affronted. "I *am* wearing pajama bottoms."

She shook her head in pity. "No, you're not."

He glanced down at his briefs and swore.

Sensing his annoyance and self-reproach Candice said, "At least you're beautifully made...I mean all over," she quickly added, making a sweeping gesture to encompass his entire body in case he misunderstood. "Not just..." She motioned to his front. "Not that I can see anything or that I would make a comment even if I could." She felt her face burn but couldn't seem to stop herself. "Because that would be inappropriate. No one should make comments about someone else's body even if it's a compliment unless—"

A twinkle of amusement lit his eyes. "Relax, Candice. I know what you mean." He walked into the kitchen. "Would you like something to drink? I've got real coffee."

"It's too late for coffee."

"I also have..." He looked briefly pained. "Herbal tea." He opened a cupboard and pulled out an enormous tin that looked as if it could make eight hundred cups of tea.

"What is that?"

"Valerin root," he said in a grave voice. "It was supposed to help with insomnia."

"Did you have to buy so much?"

"I told you I was desperate. I hate it but I can't throw it away." He pushed it towards her. "You can have it."

She pushed it towards him. "Well I'd rather not fall asleep here."

He pushed it again. "You can take it home."

She replaced it in the cupboard and closed the door. "You never know when you might need it."

The pained expression returned to his face. "I also have..." He paused, pressed a fist against his mouth as if gaining courage. "Lavender and chamomile."

Candice bit the inside of her cheek to keep from laughing at the disgust in his voice. He looked on the verge of tears. She patted him on the shoulder. "It's okay. I know how hard it is for you to admit that."

"No one can ever know."

She pressed her hand over her heart as if making a pledge. "I've seen and heard nothing. Your secret is safe."

He nodded. "Thank you."

"Besides, I don't need a relaxing drink, although it is a little distracting to talk to a practically naked man in his kitchen."

"Practically naked?" he said then followed her gaze and snapped his fingers. "Oh right, the pajamas. I knew I was forgetting something. I'll be right back."

He returned to the living room wearing checkered pajama bottoms and a black T-shirt. He held out his arms for inspection. "Better?"

"Only if you're ready to jump into bed." Somehow that sounded wrong. "I mean...So where's your bedroom?"

"Did you say you wanted something to drink?"

"No."

He tried to peer inside her large canvas bag. "What are you going to read me?"

She pushed him away then pulled out a large tome.

He took it and started to laugh. "*Robotics and Causality.* Where did you find this?"

"I was passing by a used bookstore and thought maybe..."

"That's incredible." He sat on the couch and started flipping through the pages and one would have thought she'd given him a birthday present. He groaned and pinned her with a dark look. "I told you—"

"I know. That's not what I was planning to read to you. I just found it at the back of my closet and thought I'd give it to you."

He paused. "I thought you'd found it in a used bookstore."

"Right...in a bookstore closet."

He was looking at her in that strange considering way he had that made her face burn. She reached for the book. "Let's put that away."

He moved it out of reach. "I want to look at it some more."

"It's yours. You can look at it all you want later."

"I think you wrote some notes in the margins."

She leaned closer. "I did?"

He snapped the book closed and stared at her. "So it *is* your book."

Before she had to reply, Alfonso (Oru didn't seem to fit him, she'd have to come up with another nickname) thankfully came out of hiding and meowed at her. "Hello, please help me convince your dad to go to bed with me. I mean to get in bed." She cleared her throat. "I mean, help me get your father into the bedroom." There was no way to say what she wanted to say without it sounding like a sexy invitation.

Jarell set the book down and stood. "You're sure you don't want something to drink?"

"I'm sure."

"You might get thirsty."

"I don't think I'll be here long."

"What are you going to read?"

"Get into bed and you'll find out. Sheeh. You're worse than my five year old niece."

"What's her name?"

She turned him around and shoved him forward. "Go. To. Bed."

He sighed.

"Are you nervous?"

He groaned, sounding miserable. "I know this isn't going to work."

"That kind of defeatist attitude will get you nowhere. Now come on."

Jarell stopped in front of his closed bedroom door and tugged on his ear. "I probably should warn you—"

"No more stalling," Candice said, opening the door.

Her body froze while her mind transported her back to a point in her life she'd rather forget.

CHAPTER NINE

Thoughts of her cousin flooded her mind.

Thoughts of his bright smile dimming.

Thoughts of sitting by his bedside as a nurse checked his vitals. Her memory filled with the sound of beeps and murmurs of machines, the scent of disinfectant, the taste of tears.

Jarell's bedroom had all the sterile comfort of a hospital room. It contained a bed made with military precision, a dresser drawer, and a wooden chair, which sat next to the bed and looked like one from a WWII war movie on torture.

"I know it's a little extreme," Jarell said, "but my last therapist came up with the design thinking if I had no stimulus it would help me sleep." He sat on the edge of the bed and released a sigh that made her heart ache.

She felt the stinging of tears behind her eyes as she realized he wasn't just desperate; he was dying.

Slowly. Painfully. This wasn't a game. He was dying and she had a chance to save him. In the real world there were different kinds of monsters to slay. This monster of insomnia had to be defeated.

Because Jarell had hid his pain so well, she hadn't taken it seriously. She'd found it amusing that he'd forgotten his pajamas, that he'd been late to their meeting, that he'd drawn pictures on his palm, but she didn't see those acts so simple anymore. She saw the larger picture. The shadows under his eyes, the forgetfulness, the heavy breathing. *I'm running on empty.* Those words held a new meaning. He trusted her with this secret, this battle. She pushed away the image of her cousin and swallowed determined to help him fight and win. She wouldn't fail him.

Candice sat on the rigid, uncomfortable chair. Alfonso jumped on her lap.

Jarell took him off and set the cat on the bed. "Sorry about that. He's in a strange mood tonight. He doesn't usually do that."

"You need to redecorate."

"What?"

"When you return from New York you need to change your room. It doesn't suit you. It's cold and devoid of any feeling and uncomfortable."

He stood. "I can get you another chair."

"It's not just the chair. It's everything."

He sat back down. "I thought if I only used this room to sleep in, it would help."

Candice briefly hugged herself before letting her hands fall. "It's like a prison. As if you're punishing yourself for something."

Jarell looked at her startled then shifted his gaze. "No."

She didn't believe him, but didn't want to pressure him

to reveal anymore than he felt comfortable doing, he had enough on his mind.

"I think a monastery has more flair," she said trying to soften her criticism. "I half expected to see a large cross and a flogging whip. It's okay. You don't have to explain to me, just think about it."

He sent her a curious look. "What do you think of my living room?"

"I plan to steal it when you fall asleep."

The ghost of a smile touched his lips as he got into the bed and rested against the headboard. "I thought as much."

"Lie down."

He frowned and folded his arms. "It won't make a difference."

"This is my experiment, remember? Now lie down."

He sighed then did. "Satisfied?"

"Yes." She pulled out her cell phone.

He frowned. "Where's the book?"

"I'm getting it."

"You have it on your phone?"

"Yes. I'm going to read *The Book of Tea.*"

He glared at her.

She laughed.

He shook his head. "No matter what you read, you're going to get tired scrolling."

"We'll see about that."

To her annoyance he was right. Nearly a half hour of reading *Farm Engines and How to Run Them* and he was still wide awake while she could barely keep her eyes open. She set the cell phone down in defeat. "Okay, you win."

"I know. I've listened to at least four podcasts meant to help adults fall asleep."

She shook her head and frowned at him. "It doesn't make sense. You find me more boring than farm engines?"

"It's not that I find you boring. It's just..." He paused, furrowed his brows, shook his head. "I can't explain it."

It wouldn't matter if he did. There was no pleasant way to put 'When you talk to me I feel like falling asleep'.

"Never mind. What do you want to talk about?"

"Why did you choose the name Adian?"

"I'm not going to answer that."

"Why not?"

"Try something else."

"Why did you choose your character?"

Candice shook her head. "I'm not telling you anything about the game."

"Why not?"

"Because it's important to me and it's really unnerving to share something important and then have someone snoring five minutes later."

Jarell opened his mouth as if to argue then closed it and sighed. "Fair enough. Talk about anything."

Unfortunately, her mind was blank of what to say. Like him, she had questions too. Why had the insomnia gotten worse six months ago? Was his company really in such poor condition he needed an infusion of capital? She didn't do a lot of chit chat with others so this was hard. Just talk about anything, he'd said. If only it was that easy.

He turned on his side, rested his head in his hand and lifted a velvet eyebrow. "I'm waiting."

She swallowed. "Lie back down and close your eyes."
"Why?"
Because right now you look like a cover model offering a

sexy invitation for a naughty night in bed. "Because I said so."

"Yes, Mummy."

She stuck her tongue out at him.

He laughed then fell on his back and closed his eyes. "Okay, go on."

Trivia was always a safe bet. "Cats. Let me tell you about the average length of a cat's tail..." Within minutes he was sound asleep.

She stood and winced. The chair was pure torture. She limped towards the door but turned when she heard movement. Alfonso sat and looked up at her. She pointed at the cat and mouthed, "Stay there."

But of course being a cat, Alfonso yawned, stretched and then walked across Jarell's back before leaping off the bed.

Fortunately, Jarell didn't stir.

Candice crept out of the room and gently closed the door.

The cat made a loud meowing sound.

"Shh! What is wrong with you?"

It meowed again. Louder.

She quickly opened the door a crack and the cat went back inside the room. "Make up your mind," she mumbled.

Candice softly swore and peeked inside relieved that Jarell still hadn't moved in spite of his cat's antics.

Moments later the cat returned with a toy pickle in its mouth. It dropped it at her feet.

"You want to play? Do you know what time it is?"

The cat blinked unfazed, eerily reminding her of its owner. "Five minutes."

She picked up the toy, walked into the living room then

tossed it. She sat on the couch and watched the cat chase after it. Alfonso flung the toy in the air, batted it with its paws and pounced on it. It really didn't need her, but when she stood and headed to the door it made a low growl.

"You're growling at me? Really?"

The cat sat on its haunches and licked a paw.

"I bet you're the reason for his insomnia. You're the one keeping him up, aren't you?" She knew it as a silly statement. The cat clearly wasn't a kitten and she thought only conspiracy theorist would make such a wild link but her mind did wonder why insomnia had entered Jarell's life.

Before she left, she picked up the book she'd given him and quickly flipped through it to make sure that she hadn't made any marks, before she set it down again. She was a little annoyed with herself by how happy she'd felt giving the book to him. She told herself she was just glad to give the book a good home, that it had been languishing in her closet. But it was the joy on his face she remembered. She didn't want to remember that. Not when he didn't see her. Not when she was just doing him a favor.

She turned off all the lights and left the apartment.

So her experiment hadn't worked. She couldn't get out of this. No recording, no reading boring books. He wanted her there with him to talk him to sleep.

Three nights.

She hoped they wouldn't feel like eternity.

CHAPTER TEN

*J*arell: *Told you so.*

Candice: *You don't have to rub it in.*

Jarell: *I just wanted to be sure.*

Candice: *No need for coffee today?*

Jarell: *Best sex ever.*

Jarell: *I mean* sleep. *Damn autocorrect.*

Candice: *If it's that good I should double my rates.*

Jarell: *Not a problem. What are your rates?*

Candice: *You'll find out soon enough.*

Candice: *I'm glad texting you is safe. I'd hate for you to fall asleep at the office.*

Candice: *Jarell?*

Candice: *Jarell?*

Jarell: ZZZZZ

Candice: <laughing emoji>

Jarell: *Are you free tonight?*

Candice: *I'm not coming over tonight too. Last night was just an experiment.*

Jarell: *I know. I wanted to plan this trip.*

Candice: *You can send me the details. We don't need to meet.*

Jarell: *It'll be easier that way. I have a lot to discuss. And you probably have some questions to ask me.*

Candice: *Lots but none that you'll answer.*

Jarell: *So you're fine sleeping with me?*

Candice: *Are you paying for dinner?*

Jarell: *Absolutely. Can we talk again tonight?*

Candice: *Okay.*

Candice rested her cell phone on her desk with a smile. She had a sneaking suspicion Jarell was just teasing her about their sleeping arrangements, but she wouldn't turn down a free meal or a chance to set down some ground rules. She suspected he could be sneaky when he set out to get what he wanted, but she planned to outwit him.

Candice made her way through the restaurant's crowded parking lot, the scent of batter fried onions wafting through the spring air as she got closer to the entrance. She passed by a gorgeous looking black couple standing by a blue Audi: The dark skinned woman, petite and elegant in a yellow summer dress; the man, tall and handsome in jeans, dark blue shirt and a black jacket. In the world of Flowers of Fortune and Power they'd be the kind of avatars one would create and never imagine you'd see in real life.

Candice could picture the woman with a magical sphere and the man with armor and a sword. Perhaps the woman could manipulate objects. The man could harness the elements. Even in her best pant suit Candice knew she couldn't compare. To be charitable, in her worn jacket and equally worn black shoes, she could be a side character. She didn't even have the fascinating aura of a witch. Nothing special about her. No one would choose her as a character to play online or off.

She hadn't played FFP in almost a week because of Jarell. She'd spoken to him every single night and hadn't been able to concentrate afterwards. And she'd gone out in the past several days more than she had in months. A coffee shop, his place and now a busy restaurant. It was exhausting. But one dinner to organize their plan, two weeks left before his meeting and then three nights in New York and it would all be over. She'd got back to how her life had been. Calm and drama free.

The only drama she wanted appeared in beautiful high resolution on her computer screen as it should be.

The man looked up from the woman and lifted his hand in a wave to someone behind Candice. She turned and saw three people crossing the parking lot.

She hurried forward not wanting to get in the way of their reunion.

"Stop," the man said. "Wait up."

She shoved her hands in her pockets. Funny how he sounded like Jarell. That same deep voice. But she was really thinking about him too much.

She was nearly at the door when the man raced past her and opened it. He stood aside to let her pass. "Trying to avoid me?"

She stared up at him confused. Why was he talking to her? "Do I know you?"

He frowned. "Very funny." He walked in front of her and approached the service staff.

She stood frozen. He must have mistaken her for someone else. That rarely happened but it was possible.

The man came back. "I know you don't want to do this, but I promise I won't fall asleep."

She gaped at him. No, it couldn't be.

This gorgeous looking man couldn't be Jarell.

"Why are you looking at me like that?" he said.

He looked completely different. "I didn't recognize you."

He folded his arms unconvinced.

"I'm not kidding. You look so..." Alive. She'd never realized before how ordinary he'd looked before. But now his skin glowed, his eyes shone. Was this what nearly a week of a good night's rest could do? She cupped his face in her hands. Saw his dark velvet lashes and brows. His face didn't look so angular and harsh. He was a half-dead man who'd come back to life. "I can't believe it. It really is you."

He removed her hands from his face. He mimicked her gesture, cupping her face in his hands. His large, warm hands against her skin made her pulse quicken, turned her mouth dry, she didn't have much of a chance to react when he said, "Come on. I'm hungry."

He ate like a starved man. She hardly touched her plate.

Jarell put his fork down and glared at her. "You've taken the joke far enough."

Candice blinked as if emerging from a dream. His deep voice reaching to her core. She swallowed. "Joke?"

"Staring at me like that."

"I'm staring?"

"Yes. Like you've never seen me before."

"I didn't realize you were so..."

"What?"

She wasn't going to tell him how good looking—beautiful, amazing, but most of all vibrantly alive—she found him. He wasn't conventionally handsome, but had striking, arresting features that demanded attention. He probably already knew it. He likely wouldn't have been with the woman with the Audi otherwise.

"Sorry, I just can't believe how different you look."

"I really look that different?"

He sounded truly curious, not as if he were fishing for compliments. He didn't seem the type.

"I know you told me you hadn't been able to sleep, but you looked fine to me before. Perhaps a little listless but nothing major. But now...the transformation...it's incredible."

"You really see a difference?" He picked up his fork, pushed the spiced chicken on his plate. "No one else seems to."

"That's impossible."

A smile lifted the corner of his mouth. "No, it's not. Nobody has reacted to me the way you have."

"They're probably being polite."

"Probably," he said but he didn't sound convinced. He focused on his plate. "What difference do you see?"

She sat back and studied him. "I can't explain it. But if a few nights of good sleep can change you this much you must see a new therapist."

He lowered his voice. "I think I already found one."

"Who?"

His eyes met and held hers. "You."

Her heart quickly picked up pace, Candice pushed down her excitement. His look didn't mean anything special. She was just an easy answer to a serious problem. "I'm not a therapist and I can't talk you to sleep forever. You need a proper sleep routine and a therapist can help you."

He returned his gaze to his food. "Hmm."

"You promised."

He lifted his gaze and met her eyes. "I know." It was the way he said it—like a kiss remembered, intimate, teasing—that forced her to look down, unseeing, at her own plate as heat stole into her cheeks.

He tapped the side of her plate with his fork. "You've hardly eaten anything."

She lifted up her utensils ready to dive into her brightly colored vegetable garden pasta dish. "And you haven't told me your plan."

"You're going as my girlfriend. I thought of having you as my assistant but then I'd have to explain us sharing the same room."

CHAPTER ELEVEN

Her utensils fell from her hand hitting the plate with a clatter. "We're sharing the same room?"

"Yes, how else did you expect this to work?"

"Can't there be a connecting door?"

"This is a cabin not a hotel and all the other rooms are booked. Trust me, I checked. It won't be a big deal."

"I can't be your girlfriend."

"Why not?"

"Have you looked at me?"

Jarell winked. "I'm looking at you right now."

"And you really think that you're going to convince people we're dating?"

He frowned. "Why wouldn't—"

Candice wouldn't let him finish. She didn't want to have to hear it. She held up her hand. "Here's what we're going to do. I'm your cousin um...Darius."

His brows shot up. "You want to be a guy!"

"It's better than your idea."

He stared at her open mouthed then said, "You'd rather pretend to be a *guy* than my girlfriend?"

"Seriously, my idea is more logical than yours."

"I don't see how. You're not a guy."

"I'm not your girlfriend either. For four days I'll be your cousin and assistant. No one will bat an eyelash if we share the same room. You won't have to worry about coming up with a story about us. This way we can keep our charade strictly business. I mean, if you'd thought it through, as your girlfriend not only would we have to appear like a couple, we'd have to be...affectionate."

Jarell studied her for a moment. "And that's a problem for you?" he asked in a soft, velvet tone.

Goosebumps skittered over her arms. "It's not a problem. The problem is you have zero interest in me." She held up her hand when he opened his mouth. "I'm fine with that really, but I don't want other people to see it. You literally doze off while I'm talking—"

"Not always and I won't do that there."

"Will be humiliating."

His tone hardened. "I said I won't do that."

"You don't know that."

Jarell shook his head. "No way. No one is going to believe you're my cousin Darius." He took a long swallow of his water. "I don't believe this," he mumbled under his breath.

Candice folded her arms. "Wanna bet?"

"No. Now eat your food."

"We can do an experiment."

He gritted his teeth. "No."

She clasped her hands together and leaned forward. "I'm not doing this otherwise."

He glared at her. "I said no."

He looked fierce but she wasn't deterred. She knew more than he did and if he wanted his plan to work he'd have to go with hers. "I have no curves. Front and back I'm as flat as a wall."

"You're not a wall."

"I've been mistaken for a man before. You wouldn't believe how many times I've been called 'sir'."

His jaw twitched. "So what?"

"So..." She wondered if he was being dense on purpose. "I know what I look like. I've been told I have handsome features. I have an androgynous look and voice."

"I don't care. I think you're better off playing my girlfriend—"

"I can make this work," Candice said, warming to the subject. "It will be fun. I won't interact too much, I'll stay in the room. No questions will be asked. You'll get a good night's sleep, then it will be over."

"It won't work."

"It *will* work."

Jarell shook his head. "You don't look like a guy to me."

"It's only because you know the truth. I've done it before. I'll wear my disguise."

He stared at her surprised. "You have a disguise?"

"Yes, and it doesn't take much. Let's run an experiment."

He rolled his eyes. "No."

"Please. We both know how important this meeting is to you and I consider you a friend and really want to help."

"A friend, huh?"

She rubbed her hand on her thigh. "Yes." It was hard for her to admit how important that was to her. She didn't have many. Any if she was being honest. She hoped he wouldn't reject her.

"Just a friend?" he said in a careful voice.

Oh God he knew. He knew how closed her social life was. "A...uh...close friend."

"Right." He sighed, made a low growl in his throat, reminding her of Alfonso. "How would you run an experiment?"

"We'll go some place and see what happens."

"Where?"

"Anywhere."

He narrowed his eyes. "I get to choose the place?"

"Sure," Candice said, feeling a little reckless. She liked a challenge. She picked up her knife and fork, her appetite renewed.

"Okay," Jarell said. "I'll send you an address."

CHAPTER TWELVE

"You have a mean streak," Candice said as she and Jarell stood in line, inching their way to the doors of a popular DC nightclub. An afternoon spring rain and perfume scented the air. Neon lights, shouting the club's name, pierced through the dark night.

"You said anywhere," Jarell said without apology.

Candice tugged on her dark suit. Although it was a good fit, next to Jarell's tailored jacket and crisp white shirt, she felt like a poor relation. "You could have chosen anywhere but the Razor's Edge."

"You should thank me. I'm giving you an advantage. Low lights, loud music, a crowd of people." Jarell draped an arm around her shoulders, bringing her body close to his, the scent of his cologne teasing her senses. "You should be fine 'cousin'."

She adjusted her fake black rimmed glasses and watched a woman saunter past. She flashed a shy smile at Candice.

"There will also be women on the prowl," Candice said.

Jarell affectionately patted her on the cheek. "Just make sure you're not luckier than I am."

She tried to shrug his arm from off her shoulder. "Shut up. You're enjoying this a little too much."

"We haven't even gotten started." He patted her other cheek.

She swatted his hand away. "Stop that."

"Why? We're family, remember?"

Before she could offer a rude reply, a woman touched Jarell's arm. Candice recognized the woman as the same one she'd seen standing by the Audi. "Great night, isn't it?"

"Sure," Jarell said sounding bored.

Candice noticed the woman looking at Jarell as if she wanted him to say something but he didn't appear to be interested. Candice sensed the woman wanted to be noticed. She'd taken extra care with her makeup and hair. "Do you always look this good or are you just trying to make the other ladies jealous?" Candice said.

The woman shifted her lovely gaze to Candice and beamed at her before shooting Jarell a look. "Where have you been hiding him?" Before Jarell could respond she turned back to Candice and said, "I'm Sara. Jarell's—"

"Good friend," Jarell said.

She sent him a quizzical look. He shrugged.

Candice lifted Sara's hand and bowed over it as if she were royalty. "I'm Darius. I hope we can become good friends too."

Sara laughed. "Oh, I like him."

Jarell looked vaguely annoyed but Candice was thrilled she'd made Sara smile and shown Jarell how good she was. She held up her forefinger and mouthed, "Score 1."

They made it to the door and the bouncer waved Jarell and Sara through but held out his hand to stop Candice.

"He's with me," Jarell said.

"That's fine," the bouncer said. "Let me see some ID."

Candice took out her driver's license.

She saw the man stare at her name and frown. She pointed to the date of birth. "I'm legal."

He quickly handed her ID back as if not sure what to do with it. He sent Jarell a look. "Promise there won't be any trouble."

"Why would there be any trouble?"

The bouncer met Jarell's steady gaze. "If he wants to be here and queer he'd better watch himself. It's not that kind of club."

"As I said," Jarell repeated in a quiet, steely tone, "he's with me."

The bouncer looked away and waved them through.

"Score one for me," Jarell said as Candice put her wallet away. Sara had gone ahead to secure a table.

"Only because I had to show ID."

"No, because you look like your voice hasn't broken yet."

She rubbed her chin thoughtful. "Think I should have drawn on a mustache?"

"You barely look like a college freshman. This is not going to work."

"It will work."

He led her over to a table where Sara was waiting. "What was the hold up?"

Jarell patted Candice on the back. "A minor identity crisis."

"What?"

"Never mind."

"Would you like something to drink?" Candice asked her.

"No, I'd rather dance," she said.

Candice began to sit. "Okay."

"With you."

She froze. "With me?"

"Sure." Sara held out her hand. "Don't you like to dance?"

Candice turned to Jarell in slight panic.

He looked amused. "Don't be shy." He looked at Sara, a mischievous grin on his face. "My cousin *loves* to dance."

"No, I don't—"

But Sara, being tiny and mighty, had grabbed hold of Candice's hand in a fierce grip and began pulling her towards the dance floor.

"Be gentle with him," Jarell called after them.

Sara winked at Jarell. "Don't worry I'll bring him back in one piece."

Candice glared at him. Jarell waved and smiled.

She was going into battle. That was the best way she could survive the loud music, flashing lights and crush of people. Someone brushed past her smelling like weed. She wasn't a good dancer, she could move to a rhythm that was about it. But a warrior only tactically retreated from a fight and this was one she wouldn't back down from. Jarell would surrender at all costs. Fortunately, the song was fast paced so there was no need to hold Sara.

"I'm really not a good dancer," Candice said in apology. "Jarell's just playing."

Sara smiled. "You seem to be good for him. I haven't seen him this upbeat in a while. Especially since..." Her words faded and she suddenly looked uncomfortable.

"Since..."

"You know...your cousin."

"Right," Candice said not knowing what else to say.

"I'm sorry, this isn't the place." She touched Candice's arm. "You're just my type. I like my men tall."

Candice just smiled.

Two women approached them: One with golden streaks in her long hair that matched the tight black and gold dress she wore, which looked like it had been made out of rubber. The other woman had short black hair and lashes long enough to make a butterfly jealous tipped with glitter. "Mind if we join you?"

Candice looked around as she suddenly found herself in a circle of attractive ladies. "Uh..."

"You're new here," Golden Streaks said, her words a little slurred. Candice guessed she'd been enjoying a few too many beverages.

"Jarell's cousin," Sara explained.

Glitter Lashes looked around. "Jarell's here? He hasn't been here in months."

"He's sitting alone," Candice said. "Perhaps you could keep him company. A pretty face like yours would be a welcome sight."

Glitter Lashes looked at Candice with interest. "Trying to get rid of me?"

Yes. Candice forced a laugh. "Trying my best not to make him jealous."

She looked at Golden Streaks and said, "He's adorable, isn't he?"

"He's mine," Sara said. "I promised Jarell I'd take good care of him."

"He seems fine to me," Glitter Lashes said. "You don't have to watch him."

Candice felt a certain tension, heard the tone change, and sensed if she didn't do something soon there would be an argument. She needed backup. "Let me even out this party a little," she said and headed towards the table where she saw Jarell reject the advances of a pretty woman dressed in a red skirt and silver blouse, sporting high heels as lethal as an ice pick. She marched by Candice looking miffed.

He saw Candice coming towards him. His expression remained closed and gave nothing away. He picked up a glass filled with a bright reddish liquid that looked as if it had been concocted by aliens. "You seem to be popular."

"I hate you so much right now. Get up."

"Why?"

"Because you're going to dance."

Jarell shook his head. "I don't dance."

"But you seem to be a regular here."

He shrugged. "I drink. I watch the ladies." He rested his chin in his hand. "Wanna get a drink?"

"Drop dead."

"You're really angry with me?"

"Right now I'm tempted to grab you by the collar and kiss you just to confuse the women looking at you right now."

"That would be awkward."

Candice folded her arms. "Because I'm supposed to be a guy?"

"No, because we're supposed to be first cousins. What would the family say?"

He was having too much fun with this. He was making fun of her. She couldn't return to the battle, she was spent and he was silently laughing at her. Someone she'd allowed herself to trust. But she didn't really know him. She didn't know V. Jarell wasn't V. He was just some guy who sometimes visited clubs and caught the eye of beautiful women. It hurt. She'd exposed herself and he'd taken a knife and sliced through it. She'd actually looked forward to tonight. Just like she had for their first phone call. She liked him. She liked being around him, when he managed to stay awake. But to him she was either a sleep aid or cause for amusement. Why was she such a fool?

She saw Sara coming towards them. "I'm leaving," she told him and Jarell's expression changed to alarm. He jumped to his feet.

"Wait. I'm—"

"Enjoy yourselves."

He reached for her but she moved out of reach and marched away. This was one battle she wouldn't fight. Retreat was the wisest choice.

"What did you say to him?" Candice overheard Sara say. "Why do you ruin things? No, don't tell me to be quiet. This is one of the reasons why we broke up."

CHAPTER THIRTEEN

Outside the club Candice took big gulps of air, but she still felt as if she were suffocating. She felt the stinging of tears but quickly got them under control. She wouldn't cry. She'd done an experiment and it had sobered her.

She heard hurried footsteps pounding on the pavement, felt a heavy hand on her shoulder. "Wait."

She pushed Jarell's hand away. "Leave me alone."

"I was just—"

She heard the laughter in his voice and something within her snapped. "You think this is funny? You think that I enjoy having women fawn all over me? You think I enjoy the fact that I get more attention as a man than I ever do as a woman? I wanted to help you. I know how people see me and I know how farcical it would look for you to introduce me as your girlfriend."

He stared at her in stunned disbelief. "You don't know how wrong you are."

"I know the looks I'd get."

"You don't know."

"I do because I've gotten them before." She rested her hands on her hips. "Is Sara you're ex?"

He sighed. "It's complicated."

"That wasn't my question."

"We decided to stay friends."

"So she is?"

He nodded.

"I see. So to add insult to injury you not only had to ruin our experiment in a nightclub, you had to make fun of me in front of your beautiful ex-girlfriend. I was wrong, you don't just have a mean streak. You're just cruel. Tonight you hurt me. If that's how you like to win, congratulations you won." She held up her hands. "No, don't tell me you're sorry. You're always sorry. I don't want to hear it anymore." She turned.

He jumped in front of her. "You're right. I'm an ass. But I didn't invite Sara to make fun of you. "

"Why were you talking to her at the restaurant? Did you tell her about me?"

"She doesn't know anything about you. We met by coincidence at the restaurant. She was meeting someone and I was meeting you, that's all."

"A coincidence?"

"Yes, uh...we used to go there together. The food's great."

"Right." She made a move to go past him.

He blocked her. "Candice, please I—"

"There's nothing more to say."

"I asked Sara to come tonight because... I just..." He hung his head.

"Just what?"

He lifted his head. "I needed the courage. I've been off

my game and it just felt natural to have her here too. I needed her support."

"Because you didn't want to go to a club with another 'guy'," Candice said making air quotation marks.

Jarell shook his head. "That's not what I mean."

But it made sense to her. He wanted an attractive woman by his side. She couldn't blame him for that. Candice shoved her hands in her pockets. "She still cares about you. Why did you break up?"

"We're better off as friends." He folded his arms. "How can I make it up to you?"

"You don't need to. Relax, you're not the first person to hurt me. I realize we're not really friends. Not in real life. At least we can still be virtual friends, right?"

"Candice—"

He looked miserable and sounded as if he wanted to apologize but she didn't want to hear it. "Our plan will still go forward. I'll still be your cousin for your long weekend in New York. Don't worry."

He lowered his gaze and his voice. "So I can't change your mind?"

"About what?'

He met her gaze, his eyes searching. "Pretending to be my girlfriend."

She frowned. He was still making fun of her? After all that she'd told him? She took a step back then swung at him. She meant to aim for his jaw but missed and ended up slamming her fist into his shoulder.

She felt like her hand was going to crumble into dust; he was harder than she'd thought. Tears from pain wet her eyes. She cradled her hand.

Jarell stared at her. "What was that for?"

Candice cradled her hand, she couldn't speak. That would take too much effort.

He reached out to her. "Let me see your hand. You hurt it, didn't you?"

She felt like she'd broken it but would never admit that. His ego didn't need it. She took a shaky breath and barely managed to say, "I'm fine."

"Let me see it."

"No."

"You might have sprained it."

"Don't flatter yourself."

"I'm not, I've just been in fights before and the body doesn't bounce back the way it does in video games."

Her hand felt as if it were on fire. What was the guy made out of? Steel? "I know that."

Jarell grabbed her wrist. "I bet it's already starting to swell."

Candice tried to wrestle her hand free, but ended up yelping out in pain instead.

He swore and tugged her towards him. "Don't fight me on this."

"I'm fine."

"Why did you aim for my shoulder? That is not a soft target. You should have aimed for my stomach or my groin."

She glared at him. "Don't tempt me."

He grinned. "You can be tempted, but you wouldn't succeed."

She believed him. He was not the kind of sparring partner she'd want to face in real life. In Flowers of Fortune and Power she could best him in combat, but not here. That was even more humiliating. He could both mock and beat her. He made her see how different she was from him and everyone in the nightclub painfully real. She didn't belong. She never belonged. She'd fooled herself that she could consider him a friend. She didn't have friends in the real world. She didn't need them. She had her life—her job, her game, her family and that was enough.

"Come on. Let's put some ice on this," Jarell said and then he broke through her resolve to hate him forever, by draping a protective arm around her shoulder, enveloping her in his welcoming, reassuring scent, and steering them towards the parking lot. "Let me take you home."

It was something a friend would say. It was caring.

"I can get a ride," Candice said annoyed with herself for not pulling away. He didn't care about her, but, for a brief moment, not just his words but his voice sounded as if he did.

"Exactly," he said. "With me."

CHAPTER FOURTEEN

"I thought you meant *my* home," Candice said as Jarell bandaged her hand. They sat on his living room couch with Alfonso sleeping by her feet. Jarell had removed his shoes, jacket and had rolled up his sleeves, looking completely settled in.

"My place is closer. Plus, there are a few more things we need to talk about 'cousin'."

One thing she'd learned was that Jarell was a man who liked to get his own way. She suspected he had a specific reason for her being there.

"It's close to your bedtime," she said. "You want another free session, don't you?"

Jarell looked at her surprised. "No, I wasn't thinking about that. Honestly." He finished wrapping her hand and sat back.

Candice moved to sit across from him. Being so close was uncomfortable. "So what do I need to know about you?"

"I think you already know more than enough."

She stared at him outraged. "No, I don't."

"You're my cousin. You know where I live and what I do. What else do you need to know?"

"I don't know your favorite color."

"I've never understood that question." Jarell rubbed his chin. "There are so many colors how can you have a favorite?"

"Do you have any hobbies?" Candice asked.

"How did we meet again?" He stretched his arm the length of the couch and looked at her like a king looking at a peasant. He didn't speak and she wondered if he was trying to be obtuse until she noticed the pillows on either side of him—they bore the symbol of the Flowers of Fortune and Power game. She could picture an avatar looking just like him—brown skinned, broad and a little scary with a hint of wicked sexiness.

Why did jerks have to be sexy? Candice sighed resigned. "Okay, you made your point."

Jarell's expression stilled and his gaze sharpened in that unnerving way of his when he started to study her. He leaned forward and clasped his hands together. "Candice—"

He wanted to apologize and she didn't want to hear it. She *never* wanted to hear it. "Admit I was right."

"I really didn't think it would work."

"Admit it."

He sighed. Leaned back. Picked up a pillow then set it back down and mumbled something.

Candice cupped her ear. "Again, please."

"You were right," he repeated loud enough for her to hear.

She stood. "I know. And now I should go."

"Yes, it's late." He cleared his throat. "But since you're here...."

She pointed at him. "I knew it. I knew you had a hidden agenda."

"I want to show you something."

"What?"

He headed to his bedroom.

It was the last place Candice wanted to see again, for a number of reasons. "I didn't say I'd stay."

"You don't have to stay. I said I'd take you home and I will I just wanted to show you something." Jarell opened his bedroom door then said in a soft voice, "I do consider you a friend."

His room was different. He'd worked on it. He'd listened to her. Her words had mattered to him. He'd added a standing lamp, less austere bedding but, most important, he'd changed the wooden chair and replaced it with a soft armchair. It was impractical for the room, but she knew the reason why he'd done it. He'd done it for her.

He looked at her, eager. "It's better, right?"

Candice nodded, not yet trusting herself to speak. Emotions swirling within her—she wanted to stay distant, she wanted to draw close, she wanted to stay angry, she wanted to forget everything.

"But not completely," he said, studying her face.

"It's better than before."

"Perhaps I'll take you with me next time I go shopping." He was offering her an invitation. A peace offering. He was searching for a way to apologize without words.

"Okay," she said.

She saw his shoulders relax in relief. He turned. "Now let's go."

"It's okay. I'll get a ride."

"But—"

"I'll talk you to sleep and then I'll go. This isn't an argument. I can't imagine you driving me home and then getting sleepy on the road and then crashing into a pole and injuring yourself."

Jarell tried, but failed, to suppress a smile. "That's quite an imagination."

"Get ready for bed."

"This is not why I asked you here."

"I know."

He pulled out his cell phone. "Let me get you a ride."

"I can get it myself."

He returned to the living room and sat on the couch. "I'll wait up with you."

She couldn't stop a grin. "You won't be able to do that."

He sagged into the couch and turned on the TV. "I can. How's your hand?"

She looked at her bandaged hand. "I don't know. This guy wrapped it so tight I've lost all sensation."

Jarell sat up alarmed. "Really? Let me see."

Candice laughed. "I'm kidding."

He scowled. "That's not funny."

"Then stop worrying about me, I'm fine. Besides, I should suffer for my stupidity."

He sighed. "About tonight. I—"

"Say 'I'm sorry' in any language and I'll have to smother you with a pillow."

He clicked his tongue. "So violent. Must be the video games you play."

She reached for a pillow with her good hand.

He blocked her and laughed. "Okay, okay I'll behave."

"Go to bed."

"Not until your driver comes."

"You won't be able to last five minutes."

"I will."

He lasted two. Candice helped him along to dreamland by talking throughout the show, keenly aware of when he slid down and rested his head on her shoulder.

She listened to his breathing. It reminded her of their first night. The TV had been playing in the background, just like now, and the sound of his breathing had been close to her ear. Now she had a full picture. She could now picture him on the couch with the phone resting beside him, Alfonso curled up on one side. The sounds oddly familiar and comforting.

She stiffened. Getting too used to this was dangerous. Once their New York weekend was over they wouldn't see each other again. At least not like this. He'd get a therapist and she'd go back to her game.

Her game. She hadn't played FFP for a while now and had barely missed it. That wasn't like her. She couldn't get used to this.

She gently nudged him.

"My ride is here," she lied then realized she hadn't even hailed a ride yet.

Jarell straightened and looked at her with half-closed eyes. "I'll walk you downstairs," he said sleep making his voice even deeper than usual, causing goose bumps to scatter along her skin. He stood and grabbed the back of the couch for balance, looking like a drunken man.

"No, it's fine." She took his arm and led him to his bedroom.

"But I want to make sure—"

It was sweet that he tried to care about her. "I'll send you a text when I'm in the car and when I get home, okay?"

That seemed to placate him. He stumbled, half-awake, to his bed. He slid under the covers and rested his head on the pillow. "Okay."

She pulled his sheets up to his shoulders because it seemed the right thing to do not because she had feelings for him.

"I didn't mean to hurt you," Jarell said in a velvet baritone that seemed extra soft in the stillness of the night. "I was jealous…"

Candice paused. "What?"

"Seeing you… out there… on the dance floor." His voice softened to a barely audible whisper. "I wished… I was there… too." He drifted off to sleep.

He'd been jealous? Jealous of the attention she'd been getting? That was it. That explained the look on his face. *Don't be luckier than me,* he'd said. *Jarell hasn't been here in a long time,* Glitter Lashes had said. Perhaps what had happened six months ago had affected his confidence. And then he had to see some woman, her, pretending to be a guy, getting all the female attention Jarell had wanted for himself. He'd watched her dancing with his ex and two other women. That's why there had been laughter in his voice when he'd followed her outside. He hadn't been laughing at her; he'd been covering his own disappointment. That made sense. His ego had gotten in the way.

Candice gently patted his shoulder. "There's no reason to be jealous," she said although she knew he couldn't hear her. "Once you get past this sleeping problem you'll find someone."

He'd looked so miserable at the club when he'd brushed off the attention of the woman who'd approached him. Perhaps she'd help him with that. She wasn't the most social person, but she knew how to read a scene and if she could have framed that moment she could uncover a lot more.

As successful and good looking as he was, Jarell was lonely. He craved intimacy but didn't know how to get it. It made her feel better that he hadn't thought of her as a joke, that he'd expressed his feelings. Had he lost a cousin like she had? Was that what Sara had been referring to?

Candice felt her wounded heart heal a little as she sensed a renewed bond between them. She understood loss. She wanted to help him. She liked having a sense of purpose.

She felt her heart open up. She finally understood him. She understood he had similar insecurities outside of the game world. She knew how it felt to be in control in one world and out of control in another. It no longer mattered that she still had questions about him, what had happened had created a bridge.

She crept out of his bedroom and left the door ajar a crack in case the cat couldn't make up its mind again. She was about to sit on Jarell's couch and select her ride hailing app when she glanced at his gaming station. It whispered to her.

Called to her.

Tempted her.

She couldn't overcome her curiosity. When Jarell was around she'd been embarrassed to look, but since he wasn't there...

She forgot the app and hurried over like a kid to a candy jar and sat down. She had to suppress a moan. The chair was soft, like sitting on clouds. A person could sit for hours and not feel a thing. And the keyboard was exactly what she'd suspected it to be, although the desk was beautifully designed too. She wouldn't have thought a casual user would have such a sophisticated setup. Even she hadn't gone to this level although she'd been tempted, but her bank account wept every time she thought of upgrading her home station.

But the chair.

The chair was artistry. Mastery. Even just working in her home office would be an improvement with a chair like this. She didn't envy his apartment (okay maybe a little) or job but this...this she envied to her core. Life just wasn't fair. She knew the chair was adjusted for his tall frame, but could also fit other heights. It was beautiful engineering.

Candice closed her eyes and sighed.

WHEN SHE OPENED them again she feared she'd accidently turned on the monitors. That had to be the only explanation why the room was so bright when it had been dark only seconds ago. But when she blinked, she saw that the screen was black. She felt something solid on her lap and glanced down and saw Alfonso sleeping on a blanket.

There was an indigo African textile blanket on her lap.

Where had the blanket come from? Why was it covering her?

Sizzling. Why was she hearing sizzling? And the sound of a pan scrapping against a stove? And the scent of plantain and scrambled eggs?

Someone was frying something in the kitchen. Her mouth went dry as her pulse quickened. Oh no! She'd fallen asleep. How could she have done that?

And he'd seen her like this? Sleeping in his chair? How embarrassing!

Candice gently lifted the cat from off her lap and carefully folded the blanket. She crept towards the front door hoping Jarell wouldn't hear her.

"Good, you're awake," he called out to her.

She halted with one foot lifted. Did he have cameras in the kitchen or something?

"I've got a spare toothbrush and towels for you. Take a shower and I'll have breakfast ready when you're done."

Candice lowered her foot in defeat and her stomach growled. There was no use avoiding the inevitable. A shower sounded like a good idea and the food smelled delicious. She hurried into the bathroom.

CHAPTER FIFTEEN

The man had magical powers.

That was the only way Candice could understand how Jarell had convinced her to go shopping with him.

One moment they were finishing a breakfast of heavenly soft scrambled eggs and fried plantain together (while she teased him about his strange habit of eating his scrambled eggs in a separate small bowl plus his secret tea stash) and the next moment they were walking around in a high end furniture store as if it were the most natural thing in the world.

When one of the sales reps, a man with thick, bushy brows and a pencil thin mustache, approached them and said, "How can I help you gentlemen?" Candice tossed Jarell a superior I-told-you-so grin. He didn't grin back. But she felt vindicated that her plan for the New York weekend would work.

Of course, after furniture shopping, it was only natural to grab lunch afterwards. And at lunch, when Jarell mentioned needing a new travel bag, it made sense for

Candice to help him select one and then, somehow, it was dinnertime and since they were close to a popular fast casual restaurant it made sense to get a bite to eat. And when the waitress seemed to take special interest in Jarell it only made sense to Candice to make herself scarce so that the curvy brunette got a chance to flirt with him more.

She excused herself and went to the ladies' room. She paced back and forth wondering how much time she should give the waitress to make her move. Two minutes? Five? Candice put her good hand under the water, dried it, checked her shirt in the mirror, paced some more then determined she'd given them enough time.

She left the ladies' room and halted at the sight of a big, olive toned man with an earring, an angry scowl marring his thick lips.

"Are you some sort of pervert?" he said.

"I'm sorry?"

"I got a text from my girl that you're acting funny."

Candice turned and saw an olive toned woman in a black skirt and sparkling blouse, holding her cell phone close to her chest.

"I'm not doing anything," Candice said confused.

The man grabbed the front of her shirt, twisting the fabric so it burned into her skin. "What are you doing in the ladies' room?"

"None of your business."

He shoved her against the brick faced wall with enough force she briefly saw stars. "It is my business if you're stalking women."

Candice quickly blinked, wondering how she'd get him to let go. "Stalking?"

His face was so close she could taste the barbecue sauce

on his breath. "You were walking back and forth checking out the stalls."

"I wasn't doing that! I was just pacing. Is that a crime?"

"You have no right being in there."

She wrapped her good hand around his thick wrist and struggled to get him to release her. "I have every right. I'm a woman, alright?" When he didn't let go she said, "Do you need an anatomy lesson?"

He suddenly looked unsure and she took the opportunity to dig her nails into the side of his face. He swore and shoved her away, calling her an ugly name before taking his girlfriend's hand and storming off.

Candice bent down, resting her hands on her knees and took a deep, shaky breath. *She was okay. She was okay. Everything was fine now.* She straightened and returned to the main dining area. She saw Jarell standing and looking around the room anxious, but when he spotted her he slowly sat back down. She took another deep breath and plastered on a smile.

"What took you so long?" he asked her. "Did something not agree with you? Should I complain to the chef?"

"I'm fine." Candice lifted up her utensils but her hands shook too much. She set them back down.

"What's wrong?"

Before she could reply someone bumped into the back of her chair, shoving Candice into the table. "Sorry," he muttered. She didn't need to turn around to know who it was.

Jarell's eyes flashed and he pushed his chair back, ready to attack.

Candice reached out and grabbed his hand. "It's an accident."

"It wasn't an accident."

"Leave it."

"What happened?"

She couldn't tell him. One, it was humiliating, two, it would put serious holes in her plan to play his cousin, and three, it had been an almost perfect day and she wanted it to stay that way.

"A silly misunderstanding," she said with a forced laugh. "Did you get the waitress's number? I can tell she likes you. That's good for the ego."

Jarell leaned back and tapped his forefinger on the table. "Why would my ego need that?"

He probably didn't even remember he'd told her he'd been jealous of her at the club. She didn't want him to feel bad about it. She didn't want to tread on his ego. She had to keep things nonchalant. She managed to pick up her fork and push the remainder of her grilled vegetables around on her plate, not bold enough to look at him yet. "Everyone needs an ego boost every now and then, right?"

Jarell stopped tapping his finger. She sensed him move closer, when he spoke his voice was low and tender. "Candice—"

"Really it's nothing. I'm fine." She stabbed a broccoli floret and popped it in her mouth. She swallowed and looked up at him. "Do you want to order dessert?"

He didn't, instead he asked for the bill and after Candice finished the rest of her meal they left the restaurant as the descending evening brushed the sky in a haze of colors. Candice looked up at the sky briefly wondering how she could be so ordinary in world of such beautiful things.

In the car, Jarell rested his hands on the steering wheel

before he turned to her and said, "Are you ready to tell me what happened?"

ears sprung to her eyes. No she wasn't ready, she doubted she'd ever be ready, but he had a right to know why she'd been acting strange. "I forgot okay?"

An orange hue of the descending sun touched his face, burnishing his skin, highlighting the sharp angles of his face. "Forgot what?"

"That I look like this," she motioned to her semi-disguise, the suit she'd worn to the nightclub, the glasses, "and I made some woman uncomfortable so she texted her boyfriend and he..."

Jarell's eyes turned dark. "He what?"

"Roughed me up a little."

"He touched you?"

"Nothing major," Candice quickly added, watching him grip the steering wheel in such a way she half expected him to rip it out. "I cleared it up."

He rested his forehead against the steering wheel. "Is that why you were gone so long? Some guy was—"

She waved her hands. "No, no, it happened afterwards

and it was fast. Truly. I was..." She couldn't tell him she was trying to help him get lucky. "It's been a great day, but tiring, I was gearing myself up." She added a laugh trying to soften the tension in the car. "I've never been out this much, I had to get used to it."

He straightened and stared at her. "Did he hurt you?"

"No, he just grabbed me by my collar and shoved me against the wall. If I hadn't had my hand bandaged, I wouldn't have made such an easy target," she said an attempt at humor.

Jarell didn't move. He barely blinked. He sat so silent and still Candice wasn't sure what to do.

She playfully nudged him with her elbow. "It's okay."

"Why didn't you tell me?"

"Because I handled it. Plus it was my fault for going into the ladies' room dressed like a guy. As I said, it was no big deal." She shrugged. "Pretty typical stuff when you think about it."

He looked at her amazed. "Typical?"

"Yeah. It's not the first time. It's worse when I'm not trying to be in disguise." She didn't mean to tell him the truth. She meant to make a joke and laugh it off and then change the subject instead of revealing a painful part of her history. She didn't mean to tell him she'd once had to switch schools due to bullying and a group of girls beating her up and the school saying she was at fault for the incident. She didn't mean to tell him that at another school a group of guys had given her a good pounding before they locked her in a storage closet. Neither times had she been 'in disguise', just wearing her favorite Timberlands and her cousin's sweatshirt. She didn't mean to share that by age sixteen her mother had been forced to home school her and that she'd avoided people ever since, finding it better to communicate from a distance. She didn't mean for him to know any of it but she hadn't been able to stop herself.

She didn't even realize she was crying until she felt his hand cover hers, and saw his warm tender gaze through a haze of tears.

"Next time come and get me," he said.

Candice sniffed and wiped her eyes. "It was just one guy."

"There were two people there—the man and his girl-friend. If she felt threatened that's one thing, but him assaulting you is another. Calling me would just even the score."

She shook her head. "I'd look like such a wimp."

"It takes courage to ask for help, especially when you're at a disadvantage." He lightly tapped her bandaged hand. "I'm serious. I don't care if you have to shout for me. If you won't do it for yourself at least do it for me."

Candice wiped a lingering tear from her chin and grinned and this time the grin was real because she was with Jarell and she was okay and he made her feel okay. "Why would I do it for you?"

"I was worried, all right? I was scared something had happened."

She knew that feeling, the fear of losing someone. She hadn't just lost her cousin years ago, but there had also been another person she'd thought of as a friend whose absence she felt acutely but never wanted to talk about. Loss. Her life seemed to only be about loss.

Then a realization struck her, it hadn't been about losing someone but something. He needed her for his upcoming meeting. "I'm sorry." She placed a tentative hand on his arm.

"But you don't have to worry. Nothing will happen to me before your meeting."

Jarell stared at her for a long moment before he said in a flat tone, "You think that's what worried me? Whether you can help me in New York?"

"It's okay to admit it. I know how important that meeting is to you, which makes it important to me. Nothing will ruin it."

"Right." He shook his head and said with a bit of wonder, "Unbelievable. You have no idea how..." He shook his head again and turned away.

"I do know. I know how terrifying it is to face losing something precious to you."

Jarell nodded but didn't look at her.

Candice didn't mind, he probably felt vulnerable and didn't like it. She suppressed a grin pleased that she'd managed to guess his true fear. "You can depend on me."

He took a deep breath. "I know," he said and she really wished he wouldn't say it like that. Say it with such hidden meaning as if he'd known her for years, as if they were on more intimate terms than they were. She wished those two words didn't always seem to make her skin tingle and cause her to ache to be closer to him.

She playfully nudged him in the arm with her elbow. "So tell me about the waitress."

He blinked. "Waitress?"

"You know...did she give you her number?"

He looked suddenly bored. "Hmm." He pulled out his cell phone and began scrolling through a list.

Candice leaned closer to see what he was doing. "You already exchanged numbers?"

It was when he turned to her that she realized how close she was to him. She could see the curl of his lashes.

He held her gaze and the air felt still. "No."

"Oh." She swallowed and wondered why when his gaze dipped to her lips, they tingled as if he'd kissed them with his eyes. When his gaze slipped to her neck, it felt as if he'd reached out and touched her.

He tucked his cell phone away and started the car. "Want some ice cream? I found a shop nearby."

"It's getting late."

"It's not that late."

"Can we get cupcakes instead?"

"Cupcakes?"

"Yes, I know this bakery that makes amazing cupcakes and the icing alone is heavenly."

He frowned. "I'm not really big on icing."

"Even if you take it off the rest is divine."

He drummed his fingers, pensive. "I really wanted ice cream."

"We can get ice cream another time. I think you should try this place."

Jarell sent her a curious look. "Another time? You're expecting to do this again?"

Candice hesitated, realizing the assumption she'd made. "O-only if you want to."

His face split into a wide smile lighting his eyes. He really was better looking than he should be. "I do. Next time it's ice cream. So where's this bakery?"

～

Candice sat in her desk chair and looked at the photo of her cousin and said, "And that's how I ended up spending the entire day with him. I know it's crazy, right? But it went by so fast and I helped him get a great bedroom set, but it won't be delivered until he returns from his trip, so I had him promise that he'll send me pictures. But aside from that I got to learn a lot more about him." She swung side to side in her chair. "For example, when it comes to cupcakes he's a bore. He didn't want to try anything but the vanilla ones." She stopped swinging and pointed at the picture before slapping the arm of the chair. "I know. It was almost embarrassing and then he literally scrapped off most of the icing, a complete waste. But he paid and I got two. It was great practice." That's how she planned to file away today. It was a dress rehearsal for the real thing.

She felt as if she were trying out cousin Darius with him so that it would feel natural by the time they had a real audience.

Jarell was easy to get along with and she felt less pressure being Darius than being herself. No need to worry about impressing him or being boring. He didn't care. She was useful to him and that was all that mattered. She wished there wasn't a whisper of discontent. A whisper that some-times wanted more.

CHAPTER SEVENTEEN

"*D*elivery."

"I didn't order anything," Candice told the man dressed in a light grey uniform that sported a logo she couldn't identify. She stood at her front door certain he'd come to the wrong address and opened her mouth to tell him so then looked down when her cell phone alerted her to a text.

Jarell: *Expect a delivery.*

It had been three days since she'd seen or heard from him.

Candice: *What kind of delivery?*

Jarell: *Just let them see your office and let them do the rest.*

Candice rolled her eyes and sighed before she told the delivery men, "Never mind. Bring it inside." She told them where to put the large box.

One of her roommates (the one who routinely forgot which food in the fridge was hers and which wasn't) came out of the kitchen munching on a corndog (definitely hers). "What the hell did you order?"

It took Candice a moment to realize she was talking to her. It was a rarity. "Something for my office."

Then she had an experience she'd never imagined before. She'd bought furniture before, but the care and attention she received felt as if she'd been gifted a new car.

The workers began to assemble the chair and asked her a bunch of questions. When it was completely assembled and she sat down in it, she felt as if she'd been transported.

She thanked them. Then began to text Jarell with enthusiasm but stopped herself. She wouldn't gush. She had to be cool.

Candice: *Thanks.*

Jarell: *You're welcome.*

Jarell: *Am I forgiven now?*

Candice: *You've escaped the dungeon.*

Jarell: *But not completely free?*

Candice: *I love this chair. I may never leave my house again.*

Jarell: *You still owe me a favor, remember?*

Candice: *I do?*

Jarell: *New York.*

Candice: *Oh that favor. Fine. I'll make an exception.*

THE CHAIR BECAME her new love. She didn't realize how much until the day she returned from shopping and found one of her roommates sitting in it, doing some work at her desk, eating potato chips.

"Get up!"

Her roommate spun around startled. "I didn't think you'd be back so soon—"

"Get up!"

"I spilled perfume in my room and now it stinks and I couldn't be in the living room because she was watching TV and refused to turn the volume down and I just needed a space to study so—"

"Get up!!" Candice yanked her out of her chair.

"You let me do it before."

"Once and that was when I was here. Get out."

"I'm going. I'm going."

"If I ever find you sitting in that chair again, there will be blood." When her roommate started to smile Candice narrowed her eyes. "You think I'm joking. Try me."

She hurried out of the room.

Candice felt her body tingling. It was the first time she'd stood up for herself. She usually let one of them use her place because it was neat and organized, and she didn't care. But she cared now. This chair was hers.

She carefully removed any potato chip crumbs and looked at the care instructions. The chair was more than a possession, something she could call her own, it was a gift. A gift from someone who got what she liked. Not what she was supposed to like, but really, actually liked. He understood her.

She sat down and sighed. No, she wasn't making too much of it. She just didn't like her roommate taking advantage of her anymore. She'd gotten fed up. That was all.

Candice heard the doorbell ring and then someone called out her name.

She closed her eyes. She really didn't want to be bothered right now. Whatever issue they had would pass.

Someone called her name again. Seconds later they

pounded on the door. "There's someone here to see you," one of her roommates said through the closed door.

"Me?"

"Yes."

Candice sighed and walked to the front door where she saw her two roommates staring at Jarell.

He looked pass them and waved at her. "I came to see it for myself. Pictures aren't enough."

She could see the curiosity on her roommates' faces and the silent questions. Who is this hottie? How does he know you? See what? What picture?

But that didn't matter to Candice as much as seeing that the shadows had returned to Jarell's eyes. Perhaps she should have called him every night.

"You haven't slept."

He looked surprised then flashed a quick smile. "I'm okay. It's better than before, but I'll still need you this week-end," he quickly added.

He didn't need to add that, she could tell, but she couldn't say anything more within her roommate's hearing.

"Come on," she said then led him to her bedroom and closed the door, which immediately felt like a mistake. The large room suddenly felt smaller, more cramped with him in it. She watched him look around and wondered what he was thinking of her twin size bed, the large L-shaped desk that ran along the wall then jutted out to house her workstation, a picture of one of Vincent van Gogh's many sunflowers as the screensaver, while her gaming station (bracketed by Dragon Ball figurines and the smiling face of her cousin) faced her window. Near the bookshelf, pressed against the far wall, hung two large hiking posters. One of a group hiking up a mountain that ironically said 'Get out now' and another that said 'Hiking is my therapy'.

She sensed a tension in him; he kept his hands in his pockets, his shoulders hunched, as if he wanted to make himself as small as possible so he didn't touch anything. She thought of his prison-like bedroom.

She rushed over to her new chair and hugged it, sending him a playfully fierce look. "If you've changed your mind about the chair, it's too late. I'm not giving it up."

His shoulders remained hunched but his expression softened. "I don't expect you to."

"Then what are you doing here?"

"I asked for a picture."

Candice picked up her cell phone and scrolled, searching for the image. She still remembered receiving his odd request. She'd answered immediately. "I'm sure I sent you a picture."

Jarell rubbed his forehead his voice guarded. "You did."

"See? I knew I did."

He spoke slowly. "You sent me a picture of the chair. Just the chair."

She frowned not understanding him. "That's what you wanted to see, right?"

He studied her for a moment before he hung his head, pinched the bridge of his nose and released a sigh. "Never mind." He gestured to the chair. "Sit down. I want to see you in it."

She did and ran her hands over the arm rest. She grinned, briefly closing her eyes. "It's more than a chair, it's an experience." She heard a click and her eyes flew open

She saw Jarell looking at his cell phone. She pointed at him. "Did you just take a picture?"

"Maybe."

"Why?"

He shrugged then stood beside her and held up the cell phone in front of them. "Smile."

"You want to take another one?"

"Smile."

She looked at the phone and did.

"Let me see it," she said. "I look terrible in pictures."

He tucked the cell phone away inside his jacket pocket. "You look good in this one."

"I want to see for myself."

"You'll have to take my word for it." He looked towards her desk then pointed his chin towards the photo sitting there. "Who's he?"

"My cousin. He died."

Jarell turned to her. "I'm sorry."

"Hmm...yeah...it was years ago."

Jarell's gaze didn't leave her face. "But still hurts."

Candice could only nod. She wasn't ready to talk about her cousin with anyone outside the family.

Jarell covered his mouth to hide a yawn.

She looked at him alarmed. "You are not allowed to fall asleep here."

He took off his shoes and laid down on the bed, resting on his stomach. "A quick nap."

"No."

"You said naps were good." He wrapped his arms around the pillow and buried his face in it. "Hmm it smells good...it smells like you."

"Jarell you cannot—"

"Just fifteen minutes."

"I really don't—"

"Please." He was already halfway asleep.

Candice opened her mouth to protest then decided against it. If he was asleep that left him vulnerable that meant she could try to look at his cell phone. Hopefully it hadn't gone to lock screen yet. She tipped toed and tried to slide her hand into his pocket.

Her fingers were mere centimeters away from wrapping around the phone when a large hand fastened around her wrist. He didn't open his eyes. "You don't want to do that," he said in a low warning.

"Since you're not sleeping you might as well get up."

"My fifteen minutes aren't up yet."

"You shouldn't have grabbed me then."

He loosened his hold but didn't open his eyes. "You shouldn't have tried to steal my phone."

"I wasn't trying to steal it. I wanted to look at the picture."

"If I show you, will you let me stay?"

"Don't you have somewhere to be?"

"Yes," he said with a tired sigh. "That's why a nap would help."

"How many hours have you gotten? Why didn't you call me? You know I don't mind."

"It's not just lack of sleep." He fumbled for his phone. "It's been a hard day." He pulled it out then searched and found the image he was looking for. He held it out to her.

Candice sat on the edge of the bed and looked at the image. She expected to hate it. But strangely she didn't. She looked happy. Yes, that chair really had changed her life. She looked at the second picture. "How come you're not smiling?"

"I don't smile," he grumbled. And it was when he spoke

that she realized how close she was to him. He rested on his side behind her, head in his hand. If she leaned back she could touch him.

She focused on the picture, trying not to be distracted by the scent of him, something earthly and herbal. "Yes, you do. I've seen you smile lots of times."

His voice sharpened. "Really?"

"Yes."

He leaned back, linking his hands behind his head. "I thought I'd forgotten how. I guess it only felt that way."

She picked up her cell phone and took a picture then showed him. "See? You're grinning right now."

He didn't look at the image. Instead his gaze met hers. "Because of you," he said in a soft voice, but before she could respond he took her hand. "You took off the bandage." His words were casual as was the gesture, but both made her heart lurch. But it felt strangely natural too.

It felt natural to only nod and say nothing, to lean back against him, just a little, as he seemed to study her hand as if it was something he found infinitely fascinating or even precious. It felt natural to let him briefly close his fingers around hers, and indulge in the shimmering sizzle of his touch.

He drew away before she could, glanced at the time and said, "Now I only have ten minutes," then closed his eyes.

Candice sat back in her seat and gazed at the photo surprised by how contented he looked. She set it aside. No picture could quite capture the actual man, sleeping in her bed. Although she'd seen him sleep plenty of times she couldn't seem to tire of looking at him.

He looked so much younger than when she'd first seen him. Brighter. He made her space seem brighter too.

"I forgive you," she whispered, knowing he still felt guilty about what had happened at the club.

She saw the shadow of a smile cross his face, but it happened so quickly she wasn't sure if it had been real or if she'd imagined it.

What she did know was that she couldn't wait for the weekend to come. She didn't want to grow attached to him.

More than she already was.

CHAPTER EIGHTEEN

Jarell's visit changed everything. Her roommates transformed.

Her jollof rice and spiced chicken remained untouched as well as her chocolate chip cookie ice cream. When she passed by the living room they asked her if there was anything she wanted to watch. They even asked how her day was...something they'd never done before.

Although Candice didn't share much, just about a video project she'd been working on (while she spoke one roommate checked her cell phone three times and the other yawned), it felt nice to be noticed.

Feeling good she decided to buy something new for her trip. She'd decided cousin 'Darius' would be a casual, but sharp dresser. Business casual just in case there was an unexpected meeting and Jarell needed her—him.

She went to a clothing store she and her cousin used to like to frequent, perfect for big and tall men. She was looking at a sports jacket when she looked up and saw Jarell.

His eyes widened.

Her eyes widened.

"What are you doing here?" they said in unison.

"Why wouldn't I be here?" he said.

"Because this is a store for ordinary people. Not people who can afford a chair that costs more than a luxury car payment."

"I'm an ordinary guy who likes good clothes. Now what are you doing here?"

"Shopping for Darius of course."

His face stilled. "Who's Darius?"

"Your 'cousin', remember?" She saw his face relax and briefly wondered why. He must be under a lot of stress. That worried her. She smiled, hoping to further lift his mood, and held up a shirt and jacket. "What do you think?"

"I think....it's going to be too big."

"I'm a tall guy."

"You're not a guy."

"Darius is."

Jarell sighed. "Well, *Darius* has small shoulders and... never mind. If you want to wear those," he gestured to the shirt and jacket, "you're going to need to get them tailored." He called over a sales assistant. "I want to get these two tailored and I need a suit to work for my friend here. She needs help."

"You mean he," Candice corrected.

"I mean exactly what I said."

Clothes shopping with Jarell was an entirely new experience. Although she'd visited the store with her cousin many times she'd never known the company offered a personal shopper, tailor, computerized inventory so you could look at selections at other store locations and delivery service.

And when it came to the clothing itself Candice couldn't

believe the details Jarell paid attention to as he spoke to the tailor: The cut of the shoulders, where the sleeves fell. When he had her try on a pair of trousers and two other shirts as well as another jacket she pulled him aside, "Um...this is not in cousin Darius' budget."

Jarell's expression didn't change, but she could tell he was amused. "He knows cousin Jarell likes to treat him."

"But it's just for four days."

"I know you'll find a use for them."

She blinked. "You don't mind?"

"Mind what?"

"That I might...wear this another time when I'm not Darius?"

"Why would I mind? You look good."

Candice felt oddly relieved and flattered by the compliment. He accepted her as she was. She finished getting her clothes measured and adjusted then changed into her street clothes. "Thanks," she told Jarell who had been sitting and waiting for her. "But I took up your time. You didn't get a chance to shop for yourself. What are you going to wear?"

"Maybe I'll borrow your suit."

"You'd bust through it like the Hulk."

He grimaced in good humor. "Thanks."

"It's not a criticism." She motioned to his broad build. "It's just there's more of you than me."

A smile came and went. "I know." He stood. "I'm fine. I got what I came for."

"What? I didn't see you get anything."

"I got it when you were in the dressing room."

"What?"

He hesitated then picked up the bag near his feet and pulled out two ties. They were awful. "Are they for this weekend?" Candice asked, knowing she had nothing nice to say about them. "Do you have a special occasion? Why would you need a tie for time spent in the woods?"

"It's not for this weekend. It's...for something else."

She looked at the ties again and shook her head. "No, they both won't work. This one is too thin and the wrong color. You'll look like you're wearing a leash."

"Which wouldn't be far from how it'll make me feel."

"Bet you'd rather wear a dashiki," she said referring to the colorful West African top. "Or a dark green kaftan with a matching hat."

He winked. "Absolutely."

And in an instant she imagined him looking stylish and sexy walking down a street in Lagos or Paris or New York dressed in a long, loose garment with long sleeves. "Really? You have a kaftan?"

"More than one."

"Do you have one in black?"

"Hmm."

She pressed her hands together. "My cousin used to love them too. You've got to let me see you in one someday. You must look so good."

His dark eyes studied her. "Right." He abruptly turned. "Let me pay for—"

She grabbed his arm. "I haven't forgotten about the ties."

Jarell hung his head. "Please don't torture me."

"It doesn't have to be that bad."

"I remember my mother putting on my first tie when I was three years old. Not a clip-on, a real tie that she would yank on every time I wandered off or did something wrong or annoyed her in some way."

"I'm sorry."

"I really hate ties."

"So that's why your ties are usually a mess?"

"What?"

Candice shook her head. "Never mind." She rested a hand on his arm. "What you just described was a cruel and traumatic childhood experience but neckties can be fun."

He groaned.

"I remembered one day how sharp my dad looked and begging him to show me how to tie one. My love for them began at that moment."

"It's a stupid necessity."

"No, it's not. It can be a great accessory. If this event is as important as you say then we have to select your new tie with care. Put those back."

"I already bought them."

"You can return them."

Jarell made a pitiful face. "Please don't make me. I really hate shopping for ties."

Candice bit her lip to keep from laughing. He looked adorable. "This will be fun."

He closed his eyes pained. "No, it won't."

"Yes, it will."

He sighed resigned.

She knew better than to ask for his opinion because he looked at the selection of ties with all the delight of a germo-phobe looking at mud. She finally selected a subtle grey tie and a maroon colored one. She was tempted to get one with zebra stripes but one look from Jarell changed her mind.

"See? That wasn't too painful," Candice said as they left the store. Jarell had paid for her tailored clothes to be delivered in time for her to pack them for the trip.

"No," he admitted. He pointed to the right. "My car's this way."

She pointed to the left. "And mine's that way."

"I guess I'll see you in a few days. I'll pick you up."

Her heart began to pound. It was finally happening. She was going to spend the weekend with him. "Okay."

She managed to get her wayward heart under control the morning they were supposed to leave. She carefully packed, checking twice to make sure she hadn't forgotten anything. She hadn't traveled in years. She also changed three times and finally decided on a casual pair of jeans and a salmon colored long sleeved shirt for the long drive.

She'd just watered her plants when she got a text.

Jarell: *I'm here.*

Candice took a deep breath and grabbed her suitcase. They were going to be alone in a car together and then the charade would begin.

She was excited.

She was terrified.

But when she saw Jarell standing by the open trunk of his car she was horrified.

CHAPTER NINETEEN

It took Candice a moment to realize the wailing sound of alarm wasn't just in her head, but echoed from an ambulance in the distance mixed with the high pitched yapping sound of a tiny black dog straining against its leash as its owner tried to get it under control.

"You haven't slept," Candice said.

Jarell stared at her stunned. "You can tell?"

Of course she could tell. She couldn't understand why he thought he could hide it. "How long has it been?"

He took the suitcase from her and placed it in the trunk. "I'm all right."

"When's the last time I saw you? It was only a couple days ago, right?"

"Relax. I'm okay."

But he didn't look okay. He not only looked tired, but tense. On edge.

"Are you nervous? What happened? Why didn't you call me?"

He closed the trunk of the car. "I wanted to," he said, so

softly she barely heard him.

"Has it gotten worse?"

"No. It's not...I just...it's been a hard week." He forced a humorless laugh and tried to lighten his tone, but failed. "I really need this weekend to work."

"It will work. I believe in you."

The ghost of a smile hovered over his lips, a little sad. "Thanks." He opened the backseat and grabbed a long, rectangular shaped box. "Here."

"You got me a gift?"

"It's nothing special."

Candice lifted the lid and gasped at the sight of a black velvet tie. She ran her hand over the luxurious fabric, savoring the rich feel.

"I saw you eyeing it."

Drooling more like it. She'd wanted the tie the moment she'd seen it in the store. "Thank you. I will forever treasure this." She tucked it away in her suitcase then said, "But you have to stop buying me things."

Jarell closed the trunk. "No, I don't. I like buying you things." He hesitated. "Does it make you uncomfortable?"

"No, but—"

"Then there's no problem."

"It doesn't seem fair."

"Making you happy makes me happy, okay? It's as simple as that. Now let's go."

"Fine. Give me the keys."

"Why?"

She folded her arms. "Because I plan to swallow them. Why do you think? I'm going to drive."

His jaw twitched. "I said I'm fine."

"We have more than seven hours of driving and I'm not

going to stay silent the entire time."

His tone hardened. "You don't always make me fall asleep."

She folded her arms. "You can glare at me all you want. I don't care. You're going to sit in the passenger seat and sleep then you'll be ready. Didn't you say this was important to you?"

"Yes, but—" He bit his lip then reluctantly handed her the keys. "Wake me up in an hour then I'll drive the rest of the way."

"Sure."

She didn't wake him.

When she returned to the car with a drink and sandwich she'd bought at one of the rest stops she ate and watched him sleep.

Watching him sleep also had a calming effect on her. He was like a tranquil stream. In sleep all the shadows and edges faded away. What stole sleep from him? And after this weekend what would happen between them? No, she wouldn't look that far ahead.

She had to make sure he got a good night's sleep for three nights.

Even if the thought kept her up.

YOU HAVE ARRIVED.

Candice wasn't sure to trust the GPS. After passing a large lake and rows of trees, she'd expected to happen upon a quaint log cabin. Not a massive estate home in the style of an Adirondack log cabin that looked like it had swallowed a supermarket and tripled its size, its large arched and curved windows gazing over the acres of landscaped greenery with a haughty air.

She heard Jarell shift and turned and saw him yawn and stretch. "How much farther? Ready for me to take over?"

"Absolutely. You can carry my bags."

He blinked. "What?"

"We're here. I think."

He became wide awake and looked around stunned. "We're here? You were supposed to wake me."

"I'm not sure this is the right place."

He unlatched his seatbelt. "It's the right place."

"I thought you said we were going to a cabin in the woods."

"I did."

Candice pointed to the building. "This is not a cabin."

Jarell glanced up. "It's not? What would you call it?"

"A rich man's delusion of 'roughing it'."

He laughed.

"It's enormous."

"It's sprawling, yes. It's a mixture of a hotel and B&B. More of a retreat if you like. It has a sauna and pool. "

"It could fit two Olympic size pools. How could a place like this have no internet access? I stopped the car here because just a few yards in and I lose any reception."

"It's designed that way."

"Designed?"

"The owner wants people to experience their surroundings."

Candice shook her head. "It's amazing that people will actually pay for inconvenience."

However, the greeting lounge with its high ceiling and large fireplace made her forget about any inconvenience. She felt as if she'd fallen into the seat of luxury, surrounded by the light scent of cedar wood, the sight of polished wood flooring, and smiling attendants.

She turned to ask Jarell about checking-in when she saw he stood stiff as a pillar. Something or rather someone in the lobby had caught his attention.

Candice followed his gaze and saw an attractive older black woman slowly rise from one of the chairs. She walked over to them.

Up close Candice noticed a tinge of grey in the woman's upswept hair style. She wore cotton trousers and a red blouse and had a face as sweet as marmalade. "Close your mouth, Jarell. Looking stupid and being stupid are two very different things."

And clearly a tongue as sour as vinegar.

"What are you doing here?" he said in a tight voice.

She gave him the once over. "I wanted to make sure everything went smoothly."

"It will if you don't get in my way."

Before she could say another word, a man, sitting in one of the seats in the lounge with another man opposite him, said, "Jarell! Come and join us."

"We haven't checked in yet," Jarell said by way of apology. "Perhaps later."

"Yes, yes of course."

Since they all knew each other there was no need for introductions. Aside from the coldly adorable looking woman at Jarell's side Candice instantly knew who the two men were.

Dev Chandra spoke in an accent more British than the British. Candice wasn't sure if it was affected or real. She knew she'd have more time to find out. But the accent seemed to suit the elegantly cut dark black hair, pressed trousers and black sweater. He flashed teeth so white they gleamed.

The man sitting next to him didn't smile. Candice wondered if he knew how. He stood at least four foot seven and gripped an ornate wood cane that seemed more for style than need. He wore his brown hair in a buzz cut and had an undistinguished ethnicity. If his name hadn't been Fletcher Hawkins she could imagine him speaking Spanish, Lebanese, Arabic or Italian. From what little Jarell had told her about him, Fletcher was the man to charm, the decision maker. Dev was more of a diversion.

Fletcher sent her a cool assessing look and Candice instantly liked him for it because she was just as cautious with strangers. With every person she encountered she wondered 'friend or foe' and usually relegated them to the latter. But it also surprised her that he'd take any notice of her at all. She felt uneasy prickles at the back of her neck. Would he see past her disguise? What would happen if he found out they were trying to fool them? She didn't want to ruin Jarell's chances in any way. She met his look and didn't smile back, pretending to be as cool as Adian while Dev said to Jarell, "Pleasure to see you again. Get settled in then we can talk about your trip here. Hope it wasn't too taxing."

"We haven't finished introductions," Fletcher said. "Who is this?"

Jarell turned to Candice. "This is..." He seemed suddenly frozen. Was he getting cold feet? Clearly the older woman had startled him. Fortunately, Candice was prepared for any mishaps. She cleared her throat and lifted her hand in greeting, "Hi, I'm Darius."

Jarell rested a hand on her shoulder. "My boyfriend."

CHAPTER TWENTY

There was a moment of stunned silence before Dev laughed and said something Candice couldn't hear. Her ears were ringing. The walls of the room were closing in on her.

No, that was not the plan. She was supposed to be his cousin! His *cousin!* Not his...

Had Jarell really said what she thought he'd said? Did he introduce her as his boyfriend?

"And we've really had a long journey so we'll see you later." Jarell took her arm and led her to the counter where they checked-in and got their room key. She walked in a daze. Up the stairs, down the hall, the first room to the left, it didn't matter, she wouldn't remember it anyway.

She remembered hearing a door close behind her. She walked to one of the large windows. A dark, dense forest stared back. In one level of Flowers of Fortune and Power she remembered entering a forest that looked similar. Assassins lurked behind every corner, nothing could be trusted.

The sound of birdsong could be innocent or a warning. She'd had to fight to survive.

"Candice."

Her name snapped her out of the daze. She wasn't here alone. She was here with a man. A man named Jarell.

Someone she'd meant to trust. Someone she'd wanted to trust. But he'd completely destroyed a perfect strategy. Strategy was everything when it came to survival. She spun around, any lingering feelings of shock turning to anger. "How could you do that? What is wrong with you?"

He sat at the foot of the bed.

Somehow he made the king size four poster bed look like a throne. There was no apology in his manner or stance. He sat rigid and straight with a steely control. His gaze held hers, she heard him release a breath, sharp and quick. Usually his breaths were more measured and slow, but this man was changeable. She'd never seen this side to him before.

"Nothing is wrong with me," Jarell said in an even tone that felt oddly cold in the stillness of the room. "You're the one who refused to be my girlfriend."

"What does that have to do with anything? I agreed to be your cousin."

He rubbed his chin before resting his hand on his lap. She saw it tremble a little, revealing a fissure in his veneer of control. She felt a sense of relief that he hadn't turned into a complete stranger. The Jarell she'd come to know was still there. "I didn't expect my mother to be here," he said. "I had to improvise."

"That woman is your mother?"

He flashed a sour grin. "Couldn't you sense the warm familial bond?"

His mother was deceptively cute but seemed like the

type of woman who'd secrete ice water with a touch of arsenic instead of breast milk. "I understand you were rattled but—"

"Don't you get it? I couldn't introduce you as my cousin because she'd know we were lying. Even being a distant cousin wouldn't work because she'd question it."

"I'm sure if you explained to her—"

Jarell looked at Candice for a moment then started to laugh. "That's adorable."

Even to her own ears her words sounded foolish. His mother didn't look the type to easily persuade. "Okay, you're right. Bad idea. But a boyfriend? Why couldn't I be your assistant, a trainee?"

He curled his hands into fists and rested them on his knees. "It's just for a few days, you'll be fine."

"But—"

"Sit down."

"What?"

He gestured to the space beside him. "I have to tell you something but I can't say it while facing you."

"Can't you just say it quick?"

Jarell closed his eyes. "Just sit down, please."

Candice hesitated then sat down next to him. "Okay."

He opened his eyes but his hands remained clenched into fists, his back straight like a military officer. "It will help my image, okay? It's that simple and that pathetic," he said sounding defeated. "They want to see that I'm stable and clearly having someone in your life is a symbol of that."

She jumped up and stared at him. "That's it? That's the big reveal?" He kept his gaze lowered. "Why are you looking so dejected?" She sat back down and rested a hand over his clenched hand. "If you'd have just told me that, you could have hired someone."

His eyes met hers. "I hired you."

She didn't know what affected her more, his words or his eyes. Mesmerizing brown eyes that seemed to give a deeper meaning to his words. She jumped up as if he'd burned her. "You hired me to help you fall asleep."

"Yes, but that wasn't the only reason."

She turned away from him and looked out into the forest finding more comfort in the dark unknown out there than in the room.

"I know it's a lot to ask," he said, "but I'm asking you to help me look good."

"You already look good," she mumbled.

"I'm not kidding."

She turned to him. "Neither am I. You're smart and competent."

He stood. "I've told you I've made some mistakes. I need to redeem myself. A stable relationship will help. Please."

She folded her arms. "I don't have much choice, do I?"

He rested his hands on his hips. "It won't be that bad, I promise."

"Fine." She grabbed a pillow and put it on the ground. She then opened the closet, saw an extra blanket and spread it out.

Jarell watched her. "What are you doing?"

"There's only one bed."

"I can see that."

"So I'll sleep on the floor."

His eyes flashed. "You're not sleeping on the floor."

"I don't mind."

"There's nothing to worry about between us. I'm not

going to jump you in the middle of the night and you have no interest in me. Unless..."

"Unless?"

"Unless I'm wrong."

Why would a statement like that make her mouth feel dry? Why would the expression in his eyes remind her of how much she loved and feared a summer lightning storm? Candice sensed a secret meaning hidden in a simple statement. But she wasn't in the mood to uncover it. She'd been shaken enough.

"You're not wrong," she said. "We're friends. There's nothing to worry about."

A shadow of disappointment flashed in his eyes so swiftly she wasn't sure it was real. It could have been relief. Jarell picked up the pillow and tossed it back on the bed with enough force that it hit the headboard with a bang. Clearly he didn't know his own strength or he would have tossed it with more care. "Great," he said.

His mother's unexpected arrival had really rattled him. He felt an added weight to prove himself she could understand that. She didn't want him more stressed than he already was. They were friends and friends were there for each other.

"Perhaps you should take a shower."

He turned to her a little panic. "You think I have it that bad?"

"Well, I can tell that you're stressed."

"I'm a grown man. I can handle sharing a bed."

She frowned. Why was he still harping on about the bed?

His hand wrapped around one of the posts. "I don't need a cold shower."

Candice shook her head. "I didn't say it has to be cold. It could be whatever temperature you like. Personally, I like enough heat to create steam but my sister swears on lukewarm. Says it's better for the skin. But that's completely up to you."

Jarell sighed and rubbed his eyes. "I don't need a shower."

"It could calm your nerves." She lifted her suitcase and put it on the bed. "I was going to use this tonight, but it might help." She unzipped her suitcase and pulled out a little bottle. She handed it to him.

He read the label. "Lavender oil?"

She lifted a brow. "Would you prefer lavender tea?"

He sent her a dark look.

She laughed then pointed to the bottle. "It can help with sleep. But also stress. I know you're under a lot of pressure."

He handed the bottle back to her. "You didn't have to get this for me. You're enough."

His words warmed her but she was careful not to give them too much meaning. "This is just a backup."

He looked at her suitcase and picked up her shower gel. He lifted the lid and sniffed it. "So that's your secret."

"Want to borrow it?"

"Nope. It's all yours. Don't miss a spot." He walked past her and whispered. "Use every last drop."

"Right," Candice said then hurried into the bathroom, wondering how such a simple statement could make her wish she wasn't showering alone.

CHAPTER TWENTY-ONE

She didn't use every last drop but she came close.

Every time Candice squeezed shower gel on her body brush she thought of Jarell rubbing it over her body, which was ridiculous because she didn't usually think about things like that.

She turned off the shower, dried and changed, wondering how she planned to fill the rest of the day. She opened the bathroom door then stopped halfway when she heard voices. She peeked out and saw Jarell's mother's stiff back. She could swear the temperature in the room had dropped ten degrees.

"What are you trying to do?" she heard Jarell say.

"I've already told you."

"I've explained what I plan to do. You didn't have to come."

"I wouldn't have to be here if the wrong son hadn't died. We have too much riding on this to let you do it on your own."

The cruelty of her words fell like an anvil, the silence

that followed pulsed with anger and hurt but Candice heard no movement.

"Do you think flaunting your latest fling..."

"It's not a fling."

"...in front of investors will make up for the mistakes you've made and hide your incompetence?"

"I made one mistake."

"Your brother had a wife and two kids. That's an image. What do you have? A skinny boyfriend who dresses like a college dropout. Although Sara wasn't much better, at least she was nice to look at."

"That's enough."

"He's cute, I'll give you that. What does he do anyway? Does he still live at home?"

"No and he's older than he looks."

His mother clicked her tongue. "Doesn't matter. I knew this would be a disaster."

"Nothing has happened yet."

"Precisely. If your brother were here—"

"But he's not. All you have is me. Just me. And I know how much is riding on this deal. I know that not only the future of the business but the survival of his widow and children too. Plus the employees and other members of the family. I won't let you down."

"Does your new boyfriend even have connections? I mean, if you're going to be bisexual at least have higher standards."

"You're not listening to me."

"Because you're a dreamer. You don't think rationally. You can have all the good intentions in the world, but that's not how business works. Your brother—"

Candice had heard enough. She shoved on her glasses,

pushed the bathroom door open then feigned surprise when she saw them. "Oh, I didn't know we had a visitor."

Jarell glanced at her with such pain shining in his dark brown eyes she almost gasped. She wanted to run to him. Tell him that his mother was wrong. But she had to pretend that she hadn't overheard his mother's callous words.

"Oh," his mother said, "I see you've splurged on a room with a private bath."

"I'm not charging it to the business. I'm using my own money. I had a company before being forced to save yours, remember?"

Candice heard a quick intake of breath. She sensed his mother's outrage. She knew that if she didn't intervene the scene in front of her would be verbally bloody.

She walked into the room and kept her voice light.

"Did you tell her what we've been working on? I'm his secret weapon by the way. There's a lot your company needs to focus on aside from investor money, we both know that won't save a dying ship so this is going to be a two-prong approach." She then discussed two possible made up scenario using vague business speak until his mother's eyes glazed over. She knew being boring could be useful. Now that the viper was properly defanged for the moment, Candice ended her monologue with, "And we'll share even more details later but you can be assured that if this doesn't work out Jarell has other plans in the pipeline." She looked at Jarell who'd been staring at her with a quizzical look on his face. She grabbed a scarf from her suitcase and wrapped it around her neck. "I was thinking of going for a walk, want to come along?"

Jarell looked at her tired but relieved. "Yes, that sounds good."

His mother blinked as if coming out of a haze. She opened her mouth as if to say something then changed her mind and left.

"What did you just say?" Jarell finally asked as he and Candice made their way through a path that ran parallel to the lake.

"Absolutely nothing. I just paraphrased some statements from a video script I'd once heard from a company I'd worked with. They impressed me by how they could say so much and really say nothing at all."

"You left her speechless and that's rare."

Candice sighed. "Unfortunately, I was forced to bore her. That was not how I wanted her to see me."

"Sometimes I don't think I know what I'm doing." Jarell sighed. "I really need this deal to go through."

"It will."

He fell silent then said, "I think we need to practice holding hands." He didn't look at her. He kept his gaze fixated on a flock of Canadian geese landing on the lake and she saw his jaw tense.

She opened her mouth to tease him that they didn't need to practice that and that nobody but the geese was there to see them.

"Please," he added in a soft voice.

The soft plea touched something deep within her. It made her a little angry. Angry that his mother's words could wound him so much. She felt as if she needed to do more.

But something about the way he avoided looking at her, the way he breathed, made her understand that he needed this. She slid her hand in his, feeling the warmth of his palm, then closed her fingers around his. "Tell me if it's too tight. Sometimes—"

"It's fine." His words were curt, but not dismissive. He released a deep breath. She noticed his breathing wasn't as constricted as before. It was more relaxed. She gave his hand a gentle squeeze. He didn't respond. His grip felt tight and yet not tight enough, as if he were holding back. As if he was using her as an anchor. She glanced over at him but could read nothing from his profile. He wore a mask of control.

She listened to the sound of their footsteps as they made their way along the dusty path, the sound of the wind through the trees, the intermittent squawks of the geese and in-between the tranquil sounds was his heavy laden breathing. He sounded like an old man gasping for the last pockets of air as he lay on his deathbed. The flat path shouldn't cause such difficulty for him. With every step he shouldn't sound like a man being crushed under the weight of a heavy load.

After a few moments of silence Jarell finally spoke again, but he said the words in such a rush they melded together in one long multisyllabic mess she couldn't understand.

Candice halted, forcing him to stop too. She stood in front of him, placing a hand on his chest. "Take a deep breath."

He opened his mouth to argue but the expression on her face seemed to change his mind. He closed his eyes and took a breath.

She pressed her hand against his chest again harder. "I said deep. Try again."

He swallowed then she felt his chest expand, heard the slow rush of sound leaving his mouth.

"Good. Now repeat what you said but say it slowly."

His eyes met hers. "How much did you hear?"

"Enough." She saw his shoulders slump, felt the tension return to his body. "Deep breaths."

"It's hard to look at you right now."

She returned to his side. "So don't. Let's keep walking."

Jarell fell silent and then said, "Tell me what you heard."

"I didn't hear details," Candice lied she was not going to repeat any of his mother's words. "Something about your brother."

He swallowed. Sighed. "He and my father formed the company together but he died more than a year ago. My father led the company but the grief over losing his son and the stress of running a business that was already in trouble weakened his heart. Six months ago he fell ill and had to be hospitalized. He's recovering, but still weak. He reached out to me for help...and I couldn't say no."

Pieces fell into place. His insomnia. Sara telling her how sorry she was about her 'cousin'.

"Before all this I was a simple programmer. Now, I'm the de-facto president of a company facing bankruptcy."

"If your brother was so good at what he did why is the company in trouble?"

"Because it was all a façade. My brother had two faces. One as a dutiful son, the other as a risk taker and my father let him get away with a lot. Over the past several years he'd taken a lot of risks, some paid off, most of them didn't. I'm sure before he died he thought he could have turned things around before anyone found out but he didn't have a chance. His luck ran out."

"Your mother—"

"It's her grief speaking. Someone needs to be blamed. It's nothing new."

"But that doesn't make it right. She should know the truth."

He shrugged. "To what end? All that matters is that I make sure this deal goes through."

"It will."

He sniffed. "You still believe in me?"

"Why wouldn't I?" She playfully nudged him, unable to stop a smug grin. "Plus I know another side of you that others don't."

He shoved his hands in his pockets and focused on the ground. "Yes."

"You keep me sharp."

He looked at her confused. "Sharp?"

"I've seen your gaming skills. I know you're a stellar strategist."

He threw his head back and laughed. "The game. How come I can rarely tell what you're going to say?"

"I don't know. I'm pretty boring."

He shook his head. "You're not boring."

"Says the man who—"

"You're not boring."

They walked in silence towards the lake then stopped at the bank. In the distance they could hear voices, see a group paddling across the water. Candice saw Jarell suppress a shiver. She unrolled her scarf. "Come here."

He turned to her and she wrapped the scarf around his neck. "Better?"

"Hmm. Thanks. I'll buy you a new one."

"Why don't you just buy one like it?"

He peered up at the clouds, as they slowly faded into the grey haze of the coming evening. "Because I want this one."

"There are plenty like it. It's not hard to find. There's nothing special about it."

He turned to her and said in a quiet voice, "It's special to me," then he took her hand. "It's getting late. Let's go."

CHAPTER TWENTY-TWO

It was nighttime so she must be dreaming.

Candice stood in the bathroom doorway, her mouth minty fresh after brushing her teeth, and stared at the sight facing her.

The sight of a gorgeous man wearing only black briefs standing by the side of the bed rummaging through his suitcase.

Darkness pressed against the window, letting the lamplight polish every delicious ripple and curve of his body.

Unlike her, after a late dinner, Jarell hadn't taken the time to unpack and neatly place all his folded clothes in the drawer. Instead, piles of clothes were scattered on his side of the bed. And the way he looked made her over large T-shirt no longer feel enough cover for how her body responded to him.

She heard him swear.

"What's wrong?"

"I think I forgot to pack them."

"What?"

"My pajamas."

She was not sleeping next to him dressed like that. She rushed forward determined to help him find them. "I'm sure they're here."

"I've looked."

"What's with you and pajama bottoms? Do you have the same aversion as ties?"

"No."

Candice was about to make another comment when she saw a small wooden figurine. She picked it up. "What's this?"

His face shuttered. "Nothing."

She backed away, holding it up, a grin tugging at her mouth. "Tell me."

"No."

"Come on."

"Give it back."

"Just tell me."

He became still so still that for a moment she thought he was gaining the courage to tell her what it was then he unexpectedly lunged at her with the speed of a lion.

She spun away then jumped on the bed and covered the figurine with her body.

He jumped on her back, saddling her, and tried to reach for it. "Give it to me."

She held it closer. "Is it that much of a secret?"

He tried to reach under her. "You're going to break it."

"I won't break it."

"You will!"

"Only because you weigh a ton. Get off of me."

"You shouldn't have taken it."

"I was just curious. If it breaks, which it won't, I'll buy you another one."

"You can't buy me another one," he said his voice urgent, tinged with fear.

Before she could reply, Candice heard the door swing open and then a gasp.

She turned her head and saw Jarell's mother standing in the doorway, her eyes sweeping over their position on the bed. Candice instantly became aware of Jarell's bare thighs pressed on either side of her hips, the feel of his weight on top of her butt, her exposed bare legs scattering with goose bumps from a breeze from the hallway.

"I knocked," his mother said in a weak voice that fought for nonchalance. "Clearly you didn't hear me."

Candice squeezed her eyes shut and buried her face in the blanket.

Jarell didn't move, instead she felt his sigh before he said, "What do you want?"

"It can wait for the morning." She closed the door.

"I don't think I've ever seen that expression on her face before," Jarell said amused.

Candice struggled to get out from under him. "Let me go."

"Only when you—"

"Get off me and I will."

She felt him move away, she kept her face buried in the blanket and held the figurine out to him. "Here."

He took it from her; she felt the bed shift as he sat down beside her.

She groaned. "You don't play fair."

"I didn't know she'd come in."

"What must she think of me?"

She heard laughter in his voice and felt his warm breath against her ear when he whispered, "That you love me very much."

She lifted her head and glared at him. "I'm taking my scarf back."

"I wouldn't try that."

"I could swap it out and you wouldn't know the difference."

"I'd know it." He gently placed the figurine underneath his pillow.

"Is it a lucky charm?" Candice said, motioning to the now hidden figurine.

"No."

"Meant to ward off evil spirits? Wait, no that can't be it since—" Candice abruptly stopped and bit her lip.

His gaze sharpened. "Since what?"

"Never mind."

He narrowed his eyes. "You were going to say 'since my mother is here', weren't you?"

She began to scoot off of the bed. "Let me get that lavender oil."

He grabbed her wrist, stopping her. "Does she scare you?"

"No."

"Do I scare you?"

"Why would you scare me?"

He took a deep breath, released his hold and mumbled, "Why indeed," before he got under the sheets.

SHE DIDN'T KNOW what to do with all this silence.

Plus the thought of Jarell sleeping in his briefs.

It had actually annoyed her how quickly Jarell had managed to fall asleep. She'd wanted more to do.

She sat beside him, her back against the headboard. No cell phone, no TV, no computer. She was used to staying busy. Especially at night. She didn't like to be alone with her thoughts. And what was she supposed to do all day? She'd downloaded enough music, movies and books on her tablet to keep her entertained offline, but sensed she'd get bored after a couple hours. She'd have to think of something else to do. She could come up with different ideas, different strategies to drum up new business.

She wasn't used to such quiet stillness. No place to escape.

She glanced at Jarell's sleeping face. *Do I scare you?* That's what he'd asked her with such an intense look in his eyes. "Scared of him?" Candice sniffed amused. "What a silly question."

She was more scared of herself and her growing feelings for him. He should be the one nervous. If he really knew what went on in her mind he wouldn't be sleeping so soundly. But he never had to know. Their friendship meant too much to her. *You don't have to worry about me and I don't have to worry about you.*

He had no feelings for her. He'd made her his boyfriend only because his mother was there. The handholding, keeping her scarf, it was all make believe.

One night down.

Two more to go.

CHAPTER TWENTY-THREE

She now knew what hell was like.

It was hot (no surprise there) and muggy with half-naked men.

A sweaty, half-naked Jarell was not a hellish sight, but the sight of Dev, Fletcher and some other guy with a brown beard that reached his chest and more hair on his shoulders than on his head, wasn't exactly heaven.

Candice felt the cotton towel against her bare thighs and fought not to tug on her white T-shirt (Dev had teased her about wearing it but hadn't asked questions). She found herself sitting across from Jarell after Dev had coerced her into joining him in the sauna that afternoon.

It had been a day of trials. She'd started the day determined to make sure that their stay went as seamless as possible so she made it her goal to be as kind to the staff as possible. When she saw a young woman carrying a stack of towels Candice offered to help and told her what a wonderful job she'd been doing. How much she liked the room.

She hadn't expected the woman to interpret her kindness as an invitation for her to come by the room twice, find her in the lounge chair, where Candice had been reading, and slip Candice her phone number. At breakfast when she smiled at the waitress and complimented her on her stylish shoes she didn't expect her to refill her coffee three times.

But her worst mistake, so far, was Lenora, a woman she'd found, sitting in one of the Adirondack chairs crying. Candice had asked her what was wrong and learned she'd just gotten over a breakup and was there to forget everything about her failed relationship. So Candice, naturally, sat with her and did her best to comfort the woman and tell her how amazing she was.

She never thought that Lenora would want to use 'Darius' as her rebound man. For the next hour Candice couldn't manage to get away from Lenora's unwanted attention. She managed to escape to her room but when she wanted a snack, and crept to the eating area to get some food, Lenora pounced again.

She'd been hiding underneath the stairs trying to figure out the best way to get back to her room without being detected when Dev had spotted her and told her to join him.

She'd tried to come up with every excuse she could think of but he managed to strong arm her with the promise of telling her some insights on how to charm Fletcher. He chatted in the changing room and past the pool and Jacuzzi into the small walled room of the sauna.

Jarell was just as startled (and uncomfortable) as she was when he entered the room, Fletcher barely nodded in greeting. Dev laughed and slapped her on the back. "I had a hard time convincing him to join us."

"He's shy," Jarell said.

Candice swallowed determined not to watch a river of sweat slide down Jarell's chest, how his skin glistened. Even worse, she'd been forced to remove her glasses because they'd fogged up. Initially, she'd tried to clean them, but eventually surrendered to the god of steam and hooked them on her shirt.

"I should leave you to talk business," she said.

"No, this is for relaxation," Dev said. "You look tense. Doesn't he look tense, Fletcher?"

Fletcher's keen gaze studied her. "Very tense."

"Jarell, loosen him up."

Jarell flashed a charming grin. "He's always like this."

Candice hoped she didn't pass out.

"So how did you two meet?" Dev asked.

"Online," Jarell said.

"You have to be careful there," Fletcher said. "People aren't always what they seem."

"Yes, fortunately Darius was even better than I pictured him."

"Was that the same for you?" Dev asked her.

"Yes."

Hell couldn't end soon enough, but, to her relief, it finally did with Dev and Fletcher leaving first. Candice escaped into the cooler air. She was free. She needed to change.

She shoved her glasses back on, turned the corner then saw Lenora coming out of the women's sauna down the hall, she turned to Jarell and saw him about to say her name. She covered his mouth and shoved him against the wall, her body pressed against his, her heart racing. She removed her hand from his mouth, and briefly rested her head against Jarell's shoulder hoping, praying, Lenora would just pass by without looking at them. She peeked her head around the corner. Lenora was still there talking to another woman.

She felt Jarell take a deep breath. The rumble of his voice close to her ear when he said, "What are you doing?"

"I don't want her to see us. She won't leave me alone." She felt Jarell shift and suddenly became aware of how he was responding to the situation. Her body was too, but not as evident as the bulge under his towel. She swore. Of course he'd react this way. "Oh, sorry. She really is cute, isn't she?"

His voice cracked while his eyes met hers in stunned amazement. "You think I'm like this because of *her*?"

"I'm sorry." Candice rested a hand on his chest. He really was beautifully made. Why did it have to feel so good to be this close to him? "I know I'm hot and sticky," she said, running her hand up and down his chest unable to look at him. "I'll let you go in a minute, but I'm afraid to move. She has the ears of a cat. I've told her I'm here with my boyfriend but she doesn't seem to care."

Jarell cleared his throat; briefly shut his eyes, his voice tight. "Stop...stop touching me like that."

"Touching you?"

He glanced down and she realized she'd been stroking his chest. It had felt so nice and soothing and natural that she hadn't noticed. "Sorry, nervous habit. See, when I'm at my keyboard—"

Jarell took a deep breath and she felt his entire body shake. "I don't care."

Candice patted him on the shoulder. "Don't be angry with me. I'll make it up to you."

"That's not—"

She looked again and saw Lenora headed their way. "Oh, no she's coming. I've got to run."

"You don't need to run," Jarell said then pulled her into his arms and kissed her.

She'd prepared herself for a mildly pleasant diversion. Another moment of make believe but when Jarell's lips touched hers...

Oh...pure, sweet ecstasy...

Unadulterated pleasure.

Her mind went blank. Her body came alive.

This mouth. This hot, succulent mouth...

Candice didn't remember anything else. She didn't know if Lenora passed by or saw them or stared or anything. Her heart pounded in her ears as she sank into the velvet soft kiss.

Not only did her body respond but also her heart. It whispered his name with love. But she couldn't love him. Not like this.

She began to draw back.

"Not yet," Jarell whispered against her lips. His mouth descended to her neck placing a warm, wet trail of kisses there. "We're still being watched."

She held onto him. She could hardly stand, she could hardly breathe. "Really?" she half said, half moaned.

"Really."

She could feel the butterfly softness of his lashes against her skin; she let her hands dive into the curls at the nape of his neck. Seconds felt like hours. How long could she hold on when she feared her body would burst into flames? "They're really taking their time."

"Hmm..." Jarell said his hand locking against her spine, bringing her body even closer to his. It wasn't just how he kissed, it was how he held her close, as if he'd been waiting for this moment and didn't want it to end. She could feel his uneven breathing. "They're walking...so...slowly...no, don't turn around. I'll tell you when they're gone. Trust me."

Candice swallowed. She could trust him but she couldn't trust herself. His mouth on her flesh was doing too much. She had to regain control. She cupped his face and kissed him.

A mistake. His mouth was intoxicating and she felt herself grow dizzy with lust. She let her hands explore the hollows of his back; let her tongue invade the dark, warm tunnel of his mouth. She tasted the violent hunger of her desire. She wanted to claim him.

She deepened the kiss. Deepened her exploration of him then trembled in fear when a large hand covered hers with the swiftness of a raptor. Her head snapped up and she met his eyes.

She met dark, unyielding eyes she couldn't decipher. She'd gone too far but didn't know how. She felt the fiery heat of his palm and glanced down. She held the tie of his towel in her fist. With one tug she could have had him naked. He'd been forced to stop her.

She met his eyes horrified. "I'm so sorry." She began to look behind her to see if anyone was still watching, but Jarell stopped her by placing his hand on her face and gently turning her face back to his.

"Just look at me," he said. "Otherwise it will look like a performance."

Candice lowered her gaze. "I can't look at you."

"Why not?"

"Because I'm embarrassed I got carried away."

"You're not the only one," Jarell said with a hint of regret. "I—"

She didn't want him to regret a thing. She didn't want

him to feel awkward around her. What they had was too precious. She would take all the blame. "No," she said meeting his eyes even though doing so was difficult. Even though she wanted to kiss him again. She wanted to erase the uncertainty in his gaze. He had to know he could trust her. "Don't apologize I was the one who put you in an awkward situation. I ruined your relaxing sauna and then plastered you to the wall, your legs spread apart and me pressed against you like—"

"Stop."

"What?"

"Just stop talking," he sounded pained.

She didn't blame him. What an embarrassing moment. She had to make him understand she hadn't meant for it to go this far. They still had to share a bed, she didn't want him to feel uncomfortable. "Thanks for helping me. I-I really didn't mean for it to go this far." She took a deep breath. "You don't know how much you mean to me."

This time he seemed to be the one unable to look at her. "I do." He smiled but it looked a little sad. "I really do." He pushed himself from the wall and she sensed she'd disappointed him again somehow.

And it hurt.

This was why the virtual world was better.

You were never forced to remember the lingering scent of musk and eucalyptus that seemed to cling to your skin, the burning warmth of a kiss on your lips as the man you never meant to fall in love with turned and walked away.

CHAPTER TWENTY-FOUR

Two nights left. Nothing could go wrong.

Candice walked around the perimeters of the cabin grounds, knowing she was safe after seeing Lenora drive away.

She swore. Lenora had ruined so much. She felt for Jarell. How awful it must have been for him to watch a beautiful woman chasing after his fake boyfriend.

I was jealous. That's how he'd felt at the nightclub too. But there was nothing to be jealous about. It was only because Lenora had seen her—or rather Darius—first. But with such a critical mother it didn't surprise her that Jarell's self-esteem was bruised. Plus, he had the added strain of an important business negotiation.

They were in battle together. They'd conquered the foe of insomnia. Now she'd work on his ego. He was a little too self-effacing. He needed to know how amazing he was.

Candice heard a strange sound and turned. She saw a man underneath some scaffolding that went around the back of the building near one of the windows with beautiful stone accents. She glanced up and she saw a toolbox above him shift.

A toolbox shouldn't move on its own.

Her voice caught but her body didn't, she went into a full run and tackled him before the board swung down and the toolbox crashed to the ground.

"Are you okay?" she asked the startled man.

He looked to be around her age but his wide-eyed expression made him look ten years younger. Dirt dusted his temple fade with sponge twist hairstyle and his green T-shirt had rolled up to his chest revealing well formed abs encased in pecan toned skin. He managed to nod.

Candice scrambled off him and held out her hand to help him up. "That was a lucky escape, things should be more secure. We should report—"

He jumped to his feet ignoring her outstretched hand. "No, it's my fault. Please don't say anything. I can't lose this job." She heard an accent but couldn't quite place it. He swore. "You're bleeding."

She glanced at the wound on her arm. It stung but she knew it wasn't major. "It's just a scratch." She looked around. "I really like the stone work. Especially around the sign and the one surrounding the fire pit."

"You noticed the fire pit?"

"It's amazing."

"You seem to be the only one. Most people don't see it or see it as an unnecessary extravagance."

"It immediately puts you in the right mood. I think of good friends and great memories. It fits the place. Attractive but subtle." She glanced at the impressive building. "With a place like this others would make it garish."

"Yes, that was the look I was going for."

"You succeeded."

"How come you know so much?"

She laughed. "Hardly."

"But you know something. A lot more than most."

"I had an uncle who was a brick layer."

He looked at her arm again and frowned. "We still should clean that up."

"I really don't—"

But he turned before she could finish her protest. He took her to the little shed far in the back of the property and cleaned the wound and peered closer then swore. "It looks deeper than it seems."

"Let me guess. You always wanted to be a doctor."

A quick grin came and went. "Nope, I've just watched too many medical shows."

"Well, Doctor, I think I'll be able to keep my arm."

He bandaged the wound. "We'll have to keep you under observation."

"Not too close I hope, Dr...." Candice let her words trail off hoping he'd fill in the silence.

"Reyes. Edgar Reyes."

"Darius."

"So...What are you escaping from, Darius?"

Candice stiffened, feeling suddenly exposed. Could he tell she'd been hiding from Lenora or that she'd been trying to run away from feelings that wouldn't let her go? Was it that obvious?

"Most people come to tech-free destinations for a reason," he continued.

Oh, right. Of course he wouldn't know she was trying to avoid her feelings for her fake boyfriend. "Work. A chance to think."

"Did you come alone?"

"No, I came with someone, but he's busy most of the time."

Edgar's stomach grumbled.

Candice laughed. "Looks like someone skipped lunch."

"Yeah, sometimes I lose track of time."

Candice stood. "Well, don't let me keep you."

"If you're not busy...the company would be nice."

She had nothing better to do and talking to him kept her mind off of other matters. "Sure."

THEY SAT in companionable silence by the fire pit. A slight, crisp wind carrying the chill of its mountain origins brushed through the grass enhancing the earthy scent.

"You seem like someone who has a lot on his mind," Candice finally said.

"Why do you say that?"

"You don't seem the type to make such a mistake with the scaffolding and you're eating that delicious sandwich as if it tasted like sawdust."

"Oh. No, it's good. Want some?"

"No, I'm fine. So what's on your mind?"

Edgar sighed. "It's my grandmother. She's been ill the last couple of years. I can't imagine life without her. I know it sounds stupid, she's lived a long life, but I want her around a little longer, you know? I want her to see me as a success before she dies."

"How do you know she doesn't see you as one now?"

He laughed. "My business is barely getting by, I'm living in a cheap apartment and—"

Candice shook her head. "I think you're measuring the wrong things. Have you ever shown her your work?"

"My work?"

"Yes, what you do."

He rubbed the back of his neck. "Not really. If she wants to see pictures she can go to my website."

"How old is she?"

"Eighty." He started to smile at Candice's expression. "I think I know where you're going with this."

"Yes, some seniors are techno-savvy but some would find it nice to get a picture they can hold in their hands. Not everything needs to be digital. When do you have to go home?"

"Actually I'm staying here a couple days. There's an assistants' residence a couple yards away."

"Okay, this is what we're going to do. I brought my tablet with me. I'm going to take some pictures and then email them to you. You're going to print them off and with a nice note send them to your grandmother. Let her see what you're doing now. You're right. You might run out of time so cherish every moment now."

"You'd do that for me?"

"No, I'm doing it for her." Candice ran her hand over the side of the fire pit. "When she sees what her grandson can do she's going to have some serious bragging rights. Plus her dumbass grandson doesn't realize how successful he already is."

Edgar grinned. "Dumbass?"

"Yes, if I could do even half of this I'd have an online account dedicated to my genius."

"What do you do?"

"Video editing, sometimes web design. Nothing extraordinary."

Edgar looked suddenly eager. "I could use help with my website. Unfortunately, I can't show you here since we have no WiFi."

"Don't worry," Candice said, "when I get back, I'll look it over for you. But first you'll have to look at my portfolio to make sure we're a good match."

Edgar tilted his head and softened his voice. "I don't think it'll take much convincing since I think we already are."

"A man with confidence, that's good. The key is keeping you that way. Something comes over people when they hire others."

"I know. Don't worry. I won't change. How long are you staying?"

"Just one more day. But don't worry, I'll get started on this project right away. I've got plenty of time to take good pictures so you can show your work in the best light."

SHE HAD A PROJECT! This was great. She wouldn't spend the rest of her time here thinking about Jarell. And it would give her a great way to avoid Lenora when she came back. Candice spent the remainder of the afternoon capturing as much as she could.

When it got too dark for taking any more pictures, she and Edgar had a light dinner together, the waitress watching them keenly, then sat together in the lobby. But when she saw Lenora, Candice decided to invite Edgar to her room to show him some of her ideas.

Edgar looked around the room his eyes falling on Jarell's shoes in the corner.

"You said you came here with someone?"

"Yes, my uh...boyfriend."

"Hmm. Have you been together long?"

"No, not long."

"Are you happy?"

Candice laughed at his curiosity. "That's a lot of questions. Are you worried about my heart, Doctor?"

He lifted a brow. "Maybe."

The door swung open and she heard Jarell say, "If you haven't eaten yet—," before his words died away at the sight of them.

CHAPTER TWENTY-FIVE

Candice jumped to her feet as if propelled by a rocket. Edgar remained seated. She motioned to him wondering why she felt guilty when she hadn't done anything wrong.

"Oh...Jarell. This is Edgar Reyes. Edgar, Jarell Ventura."

The two men nodded at each other but neither moved closer.

"I came to get you for dinner," Jarell said, but his gaze remained on the other man calmly sitting on the large bed.

Candice waved a dismissive hand. "Oh, you don't have to worry about that. Edgar and I already ate."

"I see." Jarell still looked at Edgar and the way he studied him Candice wondered if he thought he knew him from somewhere before. Unfortunately, she could read nothing from his tone. "What happened to your arm?"

"I'm afraid that's my fault," Edgar said.

Candice sat beside him and nudged him with her elbow. "No, it was an accident."

"It could have been prevented if I'd been more careful."

"It could have happened to anyone."

Jarell folded his arms, his voice deepened. "What happened?"

"Darius saved me," Edgar said.

"I just shoved him out of the way."

"If you hadn't been there—"

"I'm glad I was."

"Me too."

"I was going a little stir crazy."

"I know it can be hard to be alone here with few distractions."

Candice started in surprise when Jarell crossed the room and rested a heavy hand on her shoulder, his gaze never leaving Edgar's face. "Fortunately, Darius's not alone. He has me."

Edgar slowly rose to his feet, hooking his thumbs in the belt loops of his jeans. "And Darius has me when you're too busy."

Candice looked between the two men wondering why they were using Darius's name like that when 'he' was in the room.

"I'm never too busy," Jarell said.

Edgar shrugged. "Sometimes time gets away from us." He smiled at Candice. "I'll see you tomorrow. Make sure to rest your arm."

"I told you I'm fine, Doctor."

He lightly touched her arm. "And I told you I'm keeping you under close observation," he said and Candice was certain she heard Jarell growl but convinced herself she must have imagined it. "Bye," Edgar said before he left.

Jarell faced the door and slowly closed it before flattening his palms against it, keeping his back to her.

He was upset. She'd upset him again. Damn, how were they going to survive another day if she kept doing that? She searched the room, wondering what could have triggered him. She saw his note cards scattered on the dresser, she'd helped him with one of the talking points.

"Don't worry," she told him. "We didn't touch anything. I only brought him up here to hide from Lenora. Your cover isn't blown."

Jarell slowly turned. "He's a doctor?"

"What?"

"Reyes. I heard you call him 'doctor.'"

"Oh no, it's a joke. He likes medical shows. When he was bandaging my arm he was acting like a doctor. He's a really nice guy. He does all of the stone work in exchange to stay here for free. Isn't that cool? He owns his own business—"

Jarell sat down beside her. "Let me see your arm."

"It's fine. Really."

"Did you disinfect it?"

"Edgar was thorough."

"I bet he was," Jarell muttered.

"And I'm not going to unravel the bandage just so you can see my tiny wound."

"Yes, you are."

"Don't you have somewhere to be? You said you hadn't had dinner?"

He glanced at the tablet on the bed. "What were you two looking at?"

"Oh, I was taking some pictures of his work so he can send it to his sick grandmother."

Jarell's brows shot up. "A sick grandmother? You believe that?"

Candice frowned. "Yes, why would he lie about that?"

He leaned forward, covering his eyes. "Lenora. Now Edgar," he moaned.

"Relax, Edgar is nothing like Lenora. He won't cause any trouble for us. He's a really nice guy."

Jarell mumbled something.

"What?"

His hands fell to his lap. "I said you don't need to remind me."

"Then don't look so worried. Here's the best part."

He sent her a look of doubt. "There's a best part?"

"He needs a new website and wants to hire me."

Jarell folded his arms. "I see."

"Of course I told him he'd have to see my portfolio first, but he said he thinks we're already a good match."

"Hmm."

"You don't look happy for me."

"I'm over the moon."

Candice tilted her head. "Sarcasm isn't cute."

"Just be careful."

"There's nothing to be careful of. He either works as a new client or he doesn't."

"How will you explain Candice?"

"I'm sorry?"

"I'm assuming you introduced yourself as Darius. When you get back to Maryland and become Candice again how will you explain that?"

Candice fell back on the bed and swore. "I forgot about that." She snapped her fingers and sat up. "He doesn't need to know. I'll email him."

"Unless he's particularly daft the photo on your website will be a giveaway."

"I'll remove it."

"There are other photos of you online. Not a lot but enough."

Candice blinked, surprised. "You looked me up online?"

"No."

When he didn't elaborate she said, "I could lie and say I have a twin sister and she...forget it. I'll think of something."

"Probably best you don't see him again after this. If you're hurting for clients I can—"

"It's okay I don't need pity work from you. My business is fine." Candice sighed and fell back on the bed, staring up at the ceiling. "But you're probably right. Nothing that happens here should extend into my real life."

Jarell leaned down beside her, resting on his side. "I'll make time for you tomorrow."

She turned to him. He was close. So close. She was tempted to curl up against him. The teasing scent of eucalyptus reaching out to her, urging her nearer, the heat of his body, the sound of his breathing. Suddenly she remembered the touch of his sleek, smooth skin, the taste of his mouth. If she leaned a little closer...

She returned her gaze to the ceiling, her heart pounding so hard it hurt. She didn't know how she was going to sleep tonight. "No, that's okay. I know you're busy and Edgar said—"

Jarell traced a slow path up her injured arm. "I'm sorry you got hurt."

Candice fought to keep her eyes from fluttering close at the sensuous touch. If she didn't move he wouldn't stop. *Please don't stop.* "Really, it was nothing."

He traced a path down her arm. "We'll have breakfast together."

"Only if you can manage it. I know—"

He drew a circle. "I can manage it." He bit his lip. "Actually, there's something you should know." He leaned closer. "I—"

"Darius?" someone said knocking on the door. "It's me, Tami."

CHAPTER TWENTY-SIX

*J*arell looked at Candice in amazement. "Who's Tami?"

Tami continued knocking and said in a satisfied voice, "I managed to get you some—"

Candice leapt off the bed and opened the door, wanting to stop Tami before she finished her sentence. "You didn't have to do it tonight."

"You were on my mind."

Candice leaned against the door frame and smiled down at her. "I hope I didn't put you out."

She lowered her gaze, a blush touching her brown skin. "It was no trouble. I even got you some extra towels."

Candice took them from her plus some extra showering gel they'd talked about. "You're a sweetheart. Aren't you working late?"

"I wanted to make sure you were okay. What happened to your arm?"

"Oh, it's just a scratch. I—"

Jarell came up behind her. "Thanks for stopping by.

Darius really needs to get some rest. Good evening." He closed the door in the stunned woman's face.

Candice turned to him. "That was rude."

"I'm not going to sit around and watch you flirt with the staff."

"I wasn't flirting. I was being friendly."

"What did she give you?"

"Towels."

"Besides towels."

Candice flashed a smug grin, if he could have secrets so could she. "What's that little figurine represent again?"

Jarell glanced away, making it clear he wasn't going to tell her. "Is there anyone here you haven't charmed yet? I even had the waitress serving me lunch ask me about you. Who's next? The chef?"

"Oh, that's right, you said you haven't eaten. You must be hungry. Let's—"

"I've eaten. Don't change the subject."

"I don't know what you're talking about."

"Edgar, Lenora, Tami, me."

She blinked. "Yes, what about you?"

Jarell studied her. "You really don't see it, do you?"

"See what?"

He rested his hands on his hips. "I thought you didn't like people."

"I don't really but I see this all as a game."

His arms fell to his sides. "You see us as a game?"

"Not you. This." She made a vague gesture to encompass their surroundings. "It's how I survive. How I navigate life. Darius gets on well with people. That's the role I'm playing. I underestimated Lenora, but that's bound to happen. She proved a bit more of a challenge than I can handle but the others...I'm just trying to be helpful. At home I'm invisible."

"Only because you choose to be."

Candice sat on the bed. "At least Edgar doesn't find me boring."

Jarell sat down beside her. "I've never thought you were boring."

Candice couldn't hide a grin. "Says the man who could hardly keep his eyes open when we first spoke."

Jarell flexed his hand and said in a tight voice, "That was different."

"And who presently is using me as a sleep aid."

Jarell shook his head. "It's not the same. I don't find you boring. I find you...relaxing."

"So relaxing I make you fall asleep." She held up her hand. "It's okay, I understand. You're under a lot of stress. Don't worry, tomorrow I'll be back in time to talk you to sleep."

He paused. "What do you mean 'you'll be back'?"

"We're going to drive to the beach."

"Who is 'we'?"

"There's one not far from here."

"Candice. Who. Is. We?"

"Oh. Edgar and I—"

"No, you're not."

She laughed. "Cute, you sounded like you have the ability to stop me."

"You're not going."

"Why not?"

"It doesn't look right for you to go off with another man."

Candice sniffed and rolled her eyes. "Edgar is hardly 'another man'. We're friends and we won't be gone for long. I promise this won't make you look bad. In fact it will show how much you trust me. There's nothing to worry about."

"You don't know anything about him."

"He works here and he's staying here right now. I know his full name, we can check his license plate. Do you want to do a background check?"

"You just met him today. I don't think it's a good idea to go off with him."

"Stop saying it like we're two lovers running away together. It's nothing. I agreed to spend the weekend with you after one day, remember?"

"I'm different."

And he was. He'd suddenly become as dark as the forest behind them that seemed to swallow the moonlight. She couldn't read him. Something had shifted, she had to get her barings and hit upon a new strategy. This was all a game; she had to stay ahead of it. If only she could understand what she was trying to win. Was it his trust? Didn't he trust her by now? Where was his loyalty? He should know she wouldn't betray him. *I'm different.* Of course he was different. Everything was different. This room...why had it felt larger before? Why did the bed suddenly feel softer, more inviting?

How come the light seemed to draw her to every aspect of his features, the shape of his shoulders, his hands, his lips? How could she suddenly taste desire as thick and sweet as golden honey? He was different, but how she felt about him even more so. She'd never felt like this about anyone. It terrified her a little. It was irritating that he felt he had to remind her why she was there. That she was useful to him.

"You don't have to keep saying that."

"I do because I am," he said with feeling. "I've known you longer. Much longer."

"Because of the game?"

He hesitated. "Uh...yes. Including the game we've know each other a long time and you've been to my place and you've met my cat and know things about me that others don't. I don't want you falling for someone you hardly know."

"I haven't fallen for him. It will be two guys hanging out as friends."

Jarell shook his head. "He doesn't want to be friends."

"Yes, he does."

"He likes Darius." Jarell rested his hand on her thigh and slowly slid it down. "He really likes Darius."

"Oh," Candice said with a new dawning as the pieces fell into place. She felt the heat of his palm through the fabric of her jeans. Edgar liked guys. Funny she'd never thought of that.

Jarell withdrew her hand. "Why are you smiling?"

"I'm smiling?"

"Yes."

Candice tugged on her collar with a little cockiness. "I can't help it. Darius is a lucky guy." When she saw Jarell frown she laughed. "Relax. He knows I have a boyfriend."

"He doesn't care."

"You just sounded like a jealous lover."

"Maybe I am. You're supposed to be my boyfriend and not only do you have staff making after hour deliveries to you, you're planning on spending the day with another guy while I'm here working."

"It sounds really bad when you put it that way."

"There's no other way to put it!"

He reminded her of the forest, except darker, denser more dangerous. She'd done something wrong. She'd failed.

But how? She'd worked hard to make this trip a success as best she could, but Jarell was tense. Restless. Perhaps, from an outsider viewpoint, her involvement with Edgar could look bad. She didn't want anything to jeopardize his deal and she planned to talk to Dev tomorrow too, but Jarell didn't need to know about that. "You're right. I'm sorry. I can see how I'm giving him the wrong idea. And I don't want to lead him on. That wasn't my intention."

"What about me?"

"You?"

"Yes, me."

Candice paused. She rubbed her hands together until her palms started to burn. What had she missed? She could sense that she was losing his trust. He was guarding himself against her. what was this new feeling? What could Darius do that Candice couldn't? "Did something happen today? Are the negotiations not working out? Is your mother blaming you?"

Naked, stark resigned sadness shone in his eyes before he stood. "No, everything is fine."

She surged to her feet. She could face the forest and not get lost in it. Emotions usually scared her, but how Jarell felt meant too much to her to turn away, as much as she wanted to. She wanted to understand. "But you're tense about something. The truth is I'm doing this for you. Being friendly sort of gets you allies, you know? You can't fight alone. I thought if I could make things work around here it would help you. I wanted to be useful to you outside of the bedroom." She paused. "That just sounded wrong."

"I get the point," he said then paused. "You're doing this for me?"

"Yes. I know you can be particular and I thought that if I

got on the right side of the staff we could get certain privileges. For example, the extra towels didn't appear by magic. I told the waitress how you like your eggs."

A small smile softened his lips. "Hmm. I'd wondered about that."

"You got them served hot in a separate bowl, right?"

"Yes. I thought she was a mind reader."

Candice rested a hand on her chest. "You're welcome."

"Thanks for thinking of me."

Always. She smiled relieved.

He suddenly seemed less anxious, less moody. Candice wasn't exactly sure what had lightened his mood but she was glad for it. She needed space to regroup and think.

She headed to the bathroom. "I'm going to get ready for bed."

She brushed her teeth thinking of how she'd deal with the remainder of the evening. But she'd managed to calm her racing heart so that was a win. She opened the door with renewed confidence and saw a room that looked like it had been hit by a hurricane.

CHAPTER TWENTY-SEVEN

She always knew disaster could strike in minutes. But she'd never imagined it could be silent.

She hadn't heard when the four poster bed had been violently stripped naked of its bedding, which now lay pooled on the floor, or when the dresser drawers had been wretched forward at different angles and left jagged like crooked teeth. Jarell held a pillow in one hand while using the other to frantically sweep over the mattress.

"What's wrong?"

"I lost it." He put his pillow down and lifted hers.

"Your wooden figurine?"

"Yes."

"I'm sure it's here somewhere."

"Maybe Edgar took it."

"Why would Edgar take it?"

Jarell tossed the pillow on the bed. "I don't know!"

Candice told him to calm down and suggested that she'd ask Edgar and also Tami. To her regret neither had seen it.

She returned to the room and saw Jarell sitting on the side of the bed his shoulders slumped.

"I'm an idiot," he said.

"We'll find it."

"I already did." He held the small figurine out to her without turning. "I found it in a zippered compartment in my suitcase. I'd forgotten I'd put it there."

She took it and sat beside him. "Yes, you're an idiot."

"Thanks."

"Now you have to tell me what it is."

"It was my brother's. When he was young he was anxious all the time. Scared. He was about seven or eight when an uncle carved this for him. I was surprised he still had it. He used to call it..." Jarell covered his eyes.

"What?"

He groaned. "I'm too embarrassed to say it."

"You just had me searching every corner of this room, plus asking strangers about an odd little wood thing that looks between a fish and a dragon and you're too embarrassed to tell me what it's called?"

He shook his head. "I know it's stupid."

"Fine. Since you won't tell me I'll take a guess." She tapped her chin. "I bet it's called Fearsome Fear Killer."

He turned sharply to her. "That's pretty close."

She shrugged. "I was a kid too once. I had this stick that was my sword. One day, after getting the crap beaten out of me, I imagined it had magical powers that I could harness and I'd point it at people I didn't like. I looked crazy enough they left me alone."

"Do you still have the stick?"

"No."

He sighed. "I don't know why I kept it."

"Maybe because it works?" When he looked at her surprised she added, "He must have kept it all these years for a reason. Maybe there's something calming about it."

"Maybe."

She chewed her lip and hazard a guess. "And *maybe* it was yours and not your brother's." She sensed him stiffen. "And *maybe* he's the one who carved it for you and *maybe* that's why it's so special to you."

He swallowed. "Maybe."

She wondered if his hypercritical mother had anything to do with him feeling anxious all the time as a child, if she'd had a mother like his she'd have been terrified too, but she decided to keep her mouth shut. She handed the figurine back to him. "I'm glad you found it." She stood. "Now let's get this place back in order."

Jarell didn't stand. "Randall...was that his name?"

Candice felt her heart constrict. That name. That name she hadn't heard spoken aloud, now hanging in the air like a ghost. Why had he said that name? For a moment she wasn't sure she could breathe. "What?"

"Your cousin. The one who died. Was that his name?"

No, no, no. She wouldn't talk about it. She wasn't ready. "Why?"

"Was his name Randall?"

"Yes, but..." Candice let her words fade away. How would he know that? Her cousin's name hadn't passed her lips since...

"Just a couple minutes ago..." Jarell paused, sighed, tried again in a softer voice, "you called me Randall twice. You said, 'Calm down Randall.' 'It will be okay, Randall.'"

She wanted to deny it. She wanted to tell him he was

wrong, but she knew he wasn't lying. And he wouldn't have come up with that name on his own.

She fought to remain standing; she fought to keep her voice steady. "I'm sorry."

He rose to his feet. "I don't want to be a substitute."

She moved to the other side of the bed. Distance. She needed distance. And the place was a mess. They really needed to clean it up. She lifted the bed sheet from off of the floor. "You're not."

"Then what am I to you?"

"A friend?" She shouldn't have made it sound like a question but suddenly she wasn't so sure.

"What if I don't want to be your friend? What if I want to be something more?"

She continued to straighten the bed. If she ignored him perhaps he'd drop the subject. "You don't."

"What?"

"You don't know what you're saying."

"I know exactly what I'm saying. You just don't want to hear it." He got on the bed and crossed it on all fours, deliberate and slow like a parading beast of prey. She braced herself, although her head told her to retreat, she didn't move. She was in battle again. She would not cower. He could not see her fear. "I'm not going to let you hurt me again."

He studied her face. "Then why are you hurting me?"

"What?"

He sat back on his heels. "How come you feel more comfortable with me as a man than as a woman?"

She blinked quickly. "T-that's not true."

"Why didn't you want to pretend to be my girlfriend?"

"Because that would look ridiculous."

"Why?"

"You know why."

"No, I don't."

She felt her body shaking. She didn't know whether it was anger or fear. "Because I don't know how to play the role. I don't like skirts or dresses, I'm not going to bat my eyes at you and...why are you grinning like that?"

"Because I never asked you to do that. I never would."

"How would you pull it off?"

He leaned forward and removed her glasses. "I'd say, hello everyone. This is my girlfriend Candice. It seemed pretty simple to me."

She took the glasses from him and shoved them back on her face. "But it's not simple. It's easier to pretend to be someone else when I'm with you. As Darius I'm more entertaining. You...you listen to me more. Pay more attention."

Jarell shook his head. "It's not because you're pretending to be someone else."

"Candice makes you fall asleep."

He held her gaze for a long moment and looked as if he was going to say something but changed his mind. "I like you as you are," he said. "I don't want to be your cousin."

She took a step back. "You already said that."

He stood. "And I don't want to be friends."

She took another step back, bracing herself against the pain of his words. "Okay."

He rested his hands on her shoulders, halting her retreat. "I want to be more." He sighed. "I know what it's like to lose someone." He paused, gathered himself. "I gave my brother my kidney. It didn't hold. And sometimes I wonder if my mother is right—"

"No," Candice said with feeling, "she's not. Never will be."

His pain should have magnified her own but strangely it made it bearable. As he stood there the words he didn't say were just as potent as the words he did, she felt a sense of 'knowingness'. A connection of grief but also a connection of hope, of the promise of healing. The soft whisper of comfort creating an invisible bond between them.

Soon the sight of his face was obscured by a rainstorm of tears. Tears that could drown her. She felt her knees give and fell hard on the bed. She felt his arms around her and she held him tight. "I'm sorry."

"Why are you sorry?"

"I don't want to cry. This is the second time you've seen me cry. I don't usually cry in front of others."

He stroked her back. "But I'm different, remember?"

"I do." She closed her eyes, no longer feeling ashamed. She felt the most like herself when she was with him. She could even take his teasing. She told him a little about Randall and he let her talk. If she bored him, he didn't show it.

And instead of wanting to cry she wanted to laugh because talking about Randall felt so good. Jarell listened to her in a way that made her feel lucky to have known Randall. That he'd been part of her life, although the time had been shorter than they'd both wanted.

She glanced at his watch then surged to her feet. "Oh no!"

Jarell looked up at her startled. "What?"

"It's past eleven."

He looked at his watch unperturbed. "That's okay."

"You should be asleep by now. Don't you feel sleepy?"

He pulled her back down. "It's okay."

"It's not okay. Why can't you sleep?" Her mind began to race. "What if me talking to you doesn't work anymore? What if your insomnia's back?"

Jarell looked at her for a long moment. "It's not back."

He sounded so certain. "This is serious. We need to—" Candice stopped when he abruptly stood and turned his back to her.

"I have a different problem."

"You do? What is it?"

He took a deep breath. "I want to sleep with you tonight."

CHAPTER TWENTY-EIGHT

*H*e didn't turn. Didn't face her, as if preparing himself for a response he didn't want: Rejection or misdirection. But his words were clear to her because they rang true. He was asking permission. He'd told her what he'd wanted it was her turn to make the next move. She swallowed and took a step forward before she pressed her lips against the back of his neck.

Jarell spun around with the fierce, graceful speed of a lion. Shock, disbelief, hunger all flashed in his eyes, but his words remained cautious. "Are you sure?"

Candice pressed her lips against his before she said, "Are you?"

A hurricane was nothing compared to the wild desire that erupted between them. He tore off his shirt as if he'd been waiting to for days. He gathered her close and kissed her as if it had been something he'd wanted to do for even longer.

They fell on the bed. With the same efficient speed that he'd ravished the room they were both naked, she couldn't even remember where her glasses ended up. She felt her body grow wet and swollen with desire. Too soon. She was always too soon and although blood rushed through her veins, her heart pounding to the drumbeat of excitement and anticipation, she knew it would be over before the pleasure began. But she wouldn't think about that. She had to focus on him, in her mind she gauged how long it would take for him to come inside her, reach orgasm and then end. Possibly ten minutes. She knew she was being generous but Jarell wasn't like other men. She knew that men didn't like to linger long and she found the experience only barely interesting. To her, sex was basically a test of endurance and stamina. But perhaps Jarell would last a little longer than most.

"Sl-slow down," he said.

She looked at him startled. "What?"

"I said slow down. You're going a little too fast for me. I don't want to rush this. I want to enjoy it."

"You're not enjoying it?"

He ran a hand along her side. "I didn't say that. I am..." He pressed a kiss against her ribs. "So much so that I want it to last."

His breath was hot against her skin, his breathing fast. "Okay." She didn't know what that meant. This was all about objectives and goals. The goal was pleasure. Perhaps he'd last twenty minutes. She feared she wouldn't make it that long.

"You're shaking."

She didn't want to do that. Shaking was bad; shaking meant she was beginning to panic. She had to stay in control. "Do you have condoms?"

Jarell narrowed his eyes unsure. "Yes, but I was going to put it on—"

"Give me one and I can show you a trick."

He went to his suitcase then returned with one. "A trick?"

"Yes," Candice said, taking the packet. "A long time ago, when I was trying my best to be like everyone else, I was with this guy who always wanted me to go down on him. I really didn't want to but he insisted so I came up with a trick. It's a little strange and it took me a ton of practice, but what I do is—"

"Show me."

Dear God now her hands were shaking and she couldn't rip open the packet. She couldn't fail at this.

"Careful or you'll tear it."

"That's what I'm trying to do."

"I don't mean the packet, I mean the condom. We wouldn't want that." Jarell gently took the packet from her and opened it. He hesitated. "If you've changed your mind—"

Candice snatched the condom from him, her face burning. "I haven't changed my mind."

She got down on her knees, pushed his legs apart and settled between them, sitting on her heels. "Promise you won't think I'm strange."

"It's too late for that."

She smiled, not because of his joke but because he was hard. Very hard. She stared at his parted lips, feeling her trembling stop as she regained control. She had him not only ready but wanting, captivated. She watched his eyes dip to her mouth as she slowly put the condom inside before she bent her head and wrapped her lips around him. She heard him inhale sharply, the sound of his fingers scrape against the mattress as she rolled the condom on him, but not all the way. She left room so that he could feel the pressure of her tongue on him. He arched and groaned. She sucked; he moaned. He rumbled words of amazement. Mumbled words she didn't dare to believe, saying how wonderful and amazing she was. He showered her with praises that stirred her heart. She grew bolder.

He gasped. "Stop. I don't want to come."

She drew back and stared up at him confused. "I thought that was the point."

He took a deep breath. "I don't want to come like this."

"Why not?"

"Because I want to be with you."

"You're not making sense. You are. I'm right here. Let me just—"

He gripped her shoulder, stopping her, leaving her with her mouth open ready to wrap around him once more. "You're not telling me something."

She silently swore. He was really dragging this out longer than it needed to be. "There's nothing to tell."

The intense searching look, that always made her feel vulnerable, entered his dark gaze. "Have you been with a man before?"

"Of course! I've just shown you. I—"

"Not like this." He swore. "Do I really have to spell it out for you?"

"Please let me finish doing this." It seemed almost comical that she was begging on her knees. She suddenly felt so small.

He froze. Stared at her unblinking. It was as if he'd turned into an avatar of himself and his real self had abandoned the game, leaving her with no one to connect with. He left her feeling not only small but humiliated. She closed her eyes no longer able to look at him. "If you've changed your mind—"

She felt the warmth of his palm against her cheek. "I want you to enjoy it too."

"I am."

She heard him move, sensed him crouching in front of her. "Then why can't you look at me?" His hand slid to her throat. A delightful shiver swept through her. "Please look at me."

Candice opened her eyes and met Jarell's beseeching gaze. She looked at the size of his hand, the size of him and inwardly shuddered. He was so large. Big. He wouldn't mean to but all he could bring her was pain. But she couldn't hide the truth from him. "Every time I do it... it hurts." And he would hurt so much.

She bit her lip before she hung her head in shame.

"Okay, that's good news."

Her head shot up. "Good news?"

The corner of his mouth kicked up in a grin. "That means I get to take my time."

"You think that will make a difference?"

"Yes."

"B-but you're a big guy."

"I can be gentle and patient."

"Won't you get bored?"

"I won't get bored."

"What if you fall asleep?"

He gritted his teeth. "I won't fall asleep."

"You don't know that. You'll get tired waiting for me to come and then—"

Jarell stopped the rest of her words with a kiss. "I won't and you're taking up my time." He lifted her to her feet. "Let's try this again. Slowly."

Candice wouldn't have believed him if he hadn't pulled her down on the bed with him then let his gaze survey her body like a starved man. She readied herself for an assault, a sensual one but no less grasping and unpleasant. However, he surprised her by capturing one nipple in his mouth then the other. Teasing, playful. She didn't know her nipples could be so sensitive. That she could grow dizzy from his intoxicating, delicious suction.

She tried not to stiffen when he pushed her legs wide, pressing his palms on her inner thigh. She tried not to notice how large his hands were as they slid up her leg, covered her abdomen. She didn't even realize what he intended to do until she felt his fingers inside her. A smooth entrance as soft as silk. She tightened around him.

"How does that feel?" he asked her.

"I'm still afraid."

"Does it hurt?"

"No." Not yet.

"Don't close your eyes. Look at me. It's safe. I won't do anything to hurt you. If I do, you tell me and I'll stop. Deal?"

She nodded. She felt a little sorry for him. No one had been patient with her before. They'd made her feel ashamed. Made her feel as if she'd been made wrong. It was so easy for others, why wasn't it easy for her?

She felt his fingers move. Tentative and seeking.

"Still okay?"

"Yes," she breathed, feeling some of her tension ebb. This wasn't so bad. It actually was kind of...oh...ooohhh. A shock of pleasure surged through her; a pool of liquid heat startled her, her center throbbing with yearning. She squirmed and began to pull away.

"You don't like that?" he said.

"I do...it's just..."

"What?"

"I don't know."

"Don't fight it. Relax into it. No, you're getting tense again." Jarell pressed a kiss against her leg. "Trust me. Don't worry about how long it will take. I have all night. Just tell me if you want me to stop." He began to withdraw.

Candice grabbed his shoulder. "No, don't stop."

He flashed a wolfish grin. "I won't."

She waited for him to get bored, frustrated, impatient, but none of that happened and soon she truly began to not only enjoy new sensations but she began to relax. She stared at him with wonder.

"You're really enjoying this?" she said doubtful.

"I like watching you. I like you tightening around me." He kissed her stomach then deeply inhaled. "You smell so good."

He sounded sincere. He certainly looked like he wanted to devour her, but he was holding himself back. He was being so nice about this. How long had it been? He should get his turn. That was only fair. She swallowed, her throat suddenly dry. Why did he have to be so big? It was going to hurt so bad, but she'd endure it. This was probably as loose as she'd ever be. "If you want to try—"

Jarell shook his head. "No, you're not ready yet and you're getting tense again. Shh...don't think about it, don't think at all. Don't be in a rush. Just be with me and enjoy this as much as I am."

His words seemed to cast a spell. No worries, no fears.

They all melted away. Candice felt her body loosen, become more pliant. Without warning her body opened up to him, inviting him inside.

He sensed it too and their eyes met.

Held.

The smoldering heat in his gaze sent her a silent question; she licked her lip and nodded.

She tried to ignore the slight whisper of fear, of anticipated pain. If it hurt, she didn't care anymore.

"Remember the ambush?" Jarell said in a soft velvet tone, his breath warm against her ear.

She felt a rush of emotion as the memory came to life, her body pulsating, her blood racing as her mind recalled the battle Adian and V had survived—the weapons they'd used, the beasts they'd slain, the soaring music, the sounds of blades clashing, the whizzing of arrows and boom of bombs cascading around them. It was through fierce laser focus and swift action they'd managed to make it. The ambush had been one of the things they'd discussed many times in a private chat. His words made her body grow hot with the memory of a hard won victory.

"You were incredible," he said as his sleek hard body covered hers. "Amazing. Strong. Brilliant."

His words continued to cast their spell because when he entered her she felt a slight discomfort as her body adjusted to him, but no pain.

No pain. Her eyes filled with tears of relief. No pain.

There was no need to fight or fear or endure and no need to surrender. They were one. She could melt into the wild ecstasy that exploded within her with complete abandon.

And oh it...it felt so good to let go. *He* felt so good.

Sooo damnnn good. She arched her body welcoming him in deeper. Her hands swept the length of his back.

He groaned into her neck; mumbled about her beauty and power in almost worshipful tones.

She wrapped her arms around his chest, pulling him closer and told him of his magnificence, savoring every inch of him.

She'd never felt so alive outside of a game.

Her head fell to the bed, their erratic breathing filling the silence of the room. Candice nipped at his shoulder, shocked she liked the taste of someone's skin, Jarell made a guttural noise in the back of his throat.

She lightly touched his faded scar and whispered, "I'm glad you lived."

Something seemed to shatter within him, he released a sound not quite a cry or a sob but one of a wounded animal finally sensing sanctuary. He held her tight. Her body tingled and she wished she could say more but she knew there was nothing more to say.

She let him take comfort in her body as she did with his. He withdrew and reentered, each time causing her body to expand to a weightless joy taking her higher and higher until she thought she could soar.

CANDICE DIDN'T REMEMBER DRIFTING off to sleep. She didn't know when he'd left the bed or covered her with a blanket. All she knew was when she opened her eyes, the light from one lamp kept the morning darkness at bay. Jarell rested on his side looking at her.

She rubbed her eyes. "You still can't sleep?"

"I'll sleep in a minute."

"What time is it?"

"Go back to sleep."

"Do you need me to talk to you?"

He briefly pressed his forehead against hers, closed his eyes and sighed, almost wistful, before he fell back on his pillow. "Yeah."

She cleared her throat in an officious manner. "I'd hate to forget my duties."

He grinned, opened his eyes, his gaze as soft as a caress. "Told you I wouldn't fall asleep."

Heat touched her face and she felt suddenly shy. "Thanks for that." There were many more things she wanted to thank him for—his patience, his understanding—but couldn't find the words.

He poked her in the side with his finger. "I'm waiting."

"I'm thinking." She bit her lip. "How did you know?"

"About what?"

"Using the game?"

He reached up and turned off the lamp, leaving them in the faint brush of moonlight. When he spoke, the surrounding darkness made his voice seem deeper and infinitely more tender. "I don't know, it was just a feeling. A game brought us together once; I thought it could do it again."

"A clever strategy." It was more than clever it was perfect. Something special. Something only they shared. She smiled. She felt so happy she wasn't sure she'd be able to fall back asleep.

He poked her again. "You're still not talking."

"Oh, right...um..."

"Tell me what you were dreaming about."

"Dreaming?"

"Yes, just now. You were smiling."

"I was dreaming about us."

"What were we doing?"

She hesitated. "We were in a game."

He chuckled. "Why I am not surprised. I assume we were winning?"

"Yes, but at first we were locked in from all sides..."

CHAPTER TWENTY-NINE

The robe should have been a warning. But that cool spring morning Candice hadn't been in survival or battle mode so she didn't spot any signs of danger. She was still encased in the warm memory of her night with Jarell and the kiss they'd shared before he'd left to conduct some business in the city before he had a final meeting with Fletcher.

She dressed with care that morning for her meeting with Dev.

She was finally going to get some insight to help Jarell get the funding he needed.

She had a mission. She needed the right intel.

If she hadn't been so focused on her mission, she might not have so readily agreed to change their meeting place from the balcony to his suite. She also might have been more hesitant when he changed the time to a half hour early. But none of those things bothered her when she knocked on his suite door.

Not even the maroon colored robe he wore and matching

slippers. She accepted his explanation that he'd been up late and had just taken a shower. She sat across from him in the chair he gestured to, surprised by how large his suite was compared to their room. There was no four poster bed but there was a king sized bed and sitting area near a large window.

Dev smiled at her in his bright inviting way and offered her tea, which she refused. He poured himself a cup, the fragrant black tea's slightly bitter aroma wafting towards her.

"There is one major thing you need to know about Fletcher," Dev said, setting the cup down after a quick sip. "He doesn't like deception. He comes up with the idea for these retreats to see who people really are."

Candice nodded wondering why he felt he had to spell that out for her. "Right."

"It's not always easy to see one's true character. Places like this remove any distractions." He lifted his tea cup. "Don't you agree?"

"Of course."

He grinned, took another sip then carefully set the tea cup down and sat back. His friendly grin fell as did his British accent.

"So, does Jarell know that you're a woman?"

Candice didn't move not sure what shocked her more, the icy look in Dev's eyes or the fact that he sounded as if he hailed from Newark, New Jersey rather than London, England. "I'm sorry?"

"Don't insult us both by forcing me to repeat myself."

"Does Fletcher know you're not British?"

The ice in his eyes touched his lips, curving it into a superior smile. "Darling, I get to ask the questions here."

Her mind spun. This wasn't supposed to happen. How

could he suspect? She'd been so careful. Then her mind went to the changing room at the sauna. Perhaps in one of the mirrors he might have seen something she'd missed...

She could deny it. Or lie. Or both.

"He doesn't know," she said. "We haven't...known each other long."

"I see. I thought as much. Jarell doesn't seem the type. But you..." Dev wagged a finger at her, his icy smile melting into a mischievous grin. "You're a crafty one."

This wasn't happening. This wasn't supposed to happen. "What do you want?"

"Nothing much." He lifted his thumb and forefinger. "Just a little percentage of what Fletcher gives you. Nothing exorbitant. We're both adults and your little secret will stay with me for...let's say fifteen percent?"

"That's outrageous."

"Actually I think it's a bargain. But I am a fair man." He stood. "I realize it isn't completely fair to poor Jarell. So how about I drop it to ten?"

A game. This was just another game. A game she had to win. She had to remain focused. She faced serious consequences if she used the wrong tactics. She had to reveal the kind of man he was; see how far he'd go, then she could learn how to approach him.

Candice leaned forward, keeping her gaze steady. "And if I say 'no'?"

His brown eyes lit at the challenge. Yes, he was the kind of man who liked power games. Presently, he was the one who had it all. "I'll give you a third and final option. It can make this all go away. It doesn't have to be difficult."

"I'm listening."

"I'm sure there's one way you've been keeping your secret safe from Jarell but also keeping him happy." Dev dropped his rob to the floor exposing his erection. "I wouldn't mind the same service. I'm sure you've gotten far by being on your knees."

Candice slowly stood, her stomach roiling. "I'll get back to you." She walked to the door.

Dev got there before her and held it closed.

"We both know that's not how this works," he said behind her, his mouth close to her ear, the bitter taste of tea on his breath not softened by cream or sugar. "I thought you wanted to be a man. Then be one. Know when you're beaten. You can't tell Jarell about this. There's no rescuing knight, but you didn't plan to play that card did you?" She felt his cool fingers as he stroked the back of her neck. "You're used to rescuing yourself. You're in this on your own. So what are you thinking now, huh?

"Money, sex and power. That's how the world works. But you already know that. You're wondering 'What do I have?'" Dev dropped his hand from her neck and stepped back. "Jarell is so close to getting what he needs, are you going to ruin this chance for him? Or, if you're the kind of opportunist I think you are, we can come to an arrangement. I have a lot more money and connections. I can feed your greedy little heart."

Candice swallowed. Dev was not a person who believed in loyalty. He thought everyone was out for themselves, just like he was, so that was the face she'd have to show him. At least she now had a tactic she could use. She let her shoulders slump and softly swore but loud enough for him to hear her. She turned and faced him, a picture of resignation. "You're right," she said, knowing those two words would not only stroke his ego but make him more malleable. "I thought Jarell was my ticket."

His brown eyes heated. "And now?"

"I have to rethink my options." She let her gaze trail the length of him. "And they're not too bad."

He bent forward to kiss her but she turned her face away. "But I prefer money to sex. You'll get your five percent."

"I said fifteen."

"You said ten, but I'm offering you a fourth option. Why settle for money or sex when you can get both?"

Dev narrowed his eyes, greed turning his cheeks crimson. "You are a shrewd one."

"I'll need time to untangle myself after the contract is signed," Candice said, "so no false moves or I'll disappear and either Jarell signs the contract and knows nothing about this arrangement of ours or he doesn't sign the contract because *somehow* Fletcher finds out the truth. Either way you won't get anything. So you'll need to be patient if you want me to handle this."

"Agreed."

Candice picked up his robe and held it out to him. "Your tea is getting cold," she said before she turned and walked out the door.

CHAPTER THIRTY

Candice rushed down the hall, apologizing to Tami when she bumped into her and lied and told her she was fine when she asked if Candice was okay. She made it out of the building, the cool air stinging her face, and stumbled down the path along the lake then halted when she saw Fletcher sitting on a boulder. She began to turn when he called out to her. "Darius. Come. Sit with me."

That was the last thing she wanted to do but felt she had no choice.

"People think I come here for the tranquility," he said, resting his hands on the head of his cane. "But to me it reminds me that it's all an illusion. Nature is never tranquil: Under the surface of a calm lake, in the sky, in the trees, on the ground. There are always hidden battles, quests for dominance and survival. There's a beautiful butterfly desperate not to become a bird's breakfast, a fish trying not to become a hawk's dinner. Violence. All to the soundtrack of birdsong and silence." He turned to her. "You know what I mean, don't you?"

She nodded too on alert to trust herself to speak.

"You fascinate me. You're not like anyone I've ever met before."

Her heart began to pound. Had he uncovered her secret too? "I'm ordinary."

Fletcher laughed. "You're far from that. When I first saw you I wasn't sure. You had calculating eyes. Eyes of a survivor. I know. I've had to do the same. When you're overlooked, disregarded or underestimated you learn quickly what games to play to get the upper hand."

Games. He knew life was a series of games. He spoke her language, but she dare not give herself away. And, unlike Dev, there was no icy gleam in his eyes, instead they were warm almost welcoming.

But she still couldn't trust him.

"Jarell isn't like you. He's incredibly clever and shrewd, but there's a level of battle wariness he doesn't have."

"If you don't think he deserves the funding—"

Fletcher waved a dismissive hand. "He's more than qualified but I'm not here to talk about him, but about you. You know how to assess what people need, how to form alliances. That takes a certain skill. What's your endgame?"

"Endgame?"

"Are you using him?"

She paused. "You wouldn't ask me that if you really thought I was."

"Not necessarily. I'd wait for two responses: you to lie or tell the truth."

"How would you know which was which?"

He tapped the head of the cane. "I'll know when you give me a response. Are you using him?"

"No."

"That's a lie."

"No, it's not."

"You don't think it is."

"I know it."

"You're smarter than he is." Fletcher waved a hand. "Please, no false humility. We're having a chat, man to man. I've watched you. You get on with many people. Why didn't Jarell consult with you on some of his ideas?"

Candice sighed and stared out at the lake. Fletcher wasn't as clever as he thought since he was being fooled by Dev. But there were a myriad of ways Dev could have wormed his way into a partnership. She knew everyone had a weakness. "I'm just his boyfriend."

"Why?"

"I don't see why our relationship has anything to do with this."

"I'm trying to find out if Jarell is wise or foolish. Will my decision impact whether you stay or go? Of course your relationship matters. You're desperate for him to succeed. I'm a man with money and power. I know what it can do. I've seen families claw each other's eyes out, once loving spouses contemplate murder. With a 'yes' or a 'no' I can decide people's fate. I'm wondering what Jarell's will be with you."

Her mind briefly went to Dev and what she knew she had to do. "It would have nothing to do with you."

Fletcher shrugged. "Maybe."

"I think you give yourself too much credit."

"Perhaps."

"Jarell is strong and wise. He's a good man."

He tossed the cane from one hand into the other and back again. "Do you love him?"

"No."

He pointed the cane at her. "Another lie."

Candice stood. "I'm not playing this game."

"Why not? You've already won." He smiled at the look of surprise on her face. "Yes, he'll get the funding. I'll tell him when he gets back. Happy now?"

She didn't dare move sensing he had more to say.

"Forgive me, Darius. I was having a little fun at your expense." He sent her a considering look before he glanced down at this cane. "Aren't you going to ask?"

"What?"

He looked up at her. "Why I use a cane when I don't need one. Aren't you curious?"

"I assumed it was because you're vain."

Fletcher stared at her for a startled moment then threw his head back and let out a peal of laughter.

Candice wasn't sure what he found so funny. "You're a rich, good looking guy so...it made sense."

Fletcher pointed at her. "You're the first one to get it right. Most people guess I do it to look fragile or weak so that others will underestimate me, as if being under five foot isn't enough, others think I use it as a weapon." He shook his head in amazement, his eyes bright in delight. "But not you. If I wasn't married and straight..." He let his sentence fade into the pregnant silence of possibilities. "Jarell's a lucky man. I'm sure Alfonso would have liked you."

"He already does."

Fletcher frowned, confused. "I thought you'd only recently started dating Jarell."

"That's true."

"Then how did you meet his brother?"

His brother? His brother's name was Alfonso? No wonder Jarell had no intention of changing his cat's name.

Candice inwardly groaned. She felt awful for making fun of it.

"Darius? Are you okay?"

"Yes," she rubbed the back of her neck, "I—uh, thought you were talking about his cat."

Fletcher laughed again. "You're funny."

She wasn't trying to be. "I should go."

"Not before I thank you."

That came out of nowhere. "Thank me? Why?"

"For Edgar."

She sat down. "Edgar?"

He nodded. "Yes, my nephew. I was worried about him, that's why I had him up here. The entire family was. My sister reached out to me but I knew I could only do so much. He had to find his way, but within a day of talking to you he's changed. He has a spring in his step, more confidence. You're good."

"I didn't know he was your nephew."

"You weren't meant to know. That's what impressed me even more. You helped him just because you could." Fletcher stood, patted her on the shoulder. "If you ever need a favor let me know. You're an honest man. That should be rewarded."

Honest.

Her mouth felt dry as she stared out at the lake. She'd lied to them all. Revealing her disguise would be a betrayal to him and Edgar and others who'd trusted her. She couldn't tell Fletcher about Dev. She couldn't tell Jarell either. She couldn't tell anyone.

That evening Candice pasted on a smile when Jarell burst through the doors with the news she'd expected to hear.

The bright smile on his face nearly broke her heart. He was happy, relieved. The burden lifted.

She couldn't tell him the truth. He needed the funding. He could stand tall in front of his mother. Everything was depending on this. On her. The smile on his face, she couldn't take it away.

"I knew you could do it," she said.

Jarell pulled her into his arms and hugged her. "I couldn't have done it without you."

"But I didn't—"

He kissed her protests away and she let him, while fighting back tears.

He drew away and laughed. "You're so happy you want to cry?"

Candice nodded, wiping away a stray tear. "Sorry. I was a little worried that it might not work and now I'm so relieved."

"So you lied."

"What?"

"You didn't really believe in me."

"No, that's not it. I didn't believe it'd be enough to have me here."

He tenderly cupped her face. "I'm glad you came."

"Tell me what happened." She sat on the bed and listened as he talked. She'd never seen him so animated. She let him get ready for bed first then followed after him, brushing her teeth until her gums felt they were on fire. She rinsed out her mouth and returned to the room. "So what do you want me to talk—" The rest of her words caught in her throat as her mind fought to deny the sight she'd secretly feared.

Jarell lay fast asleep.

He'd fallen asleep without her.
Her greatest fear had come true.
He had his funding.
His life was back in order.
He could sleep now.
He didn't need her anymore.

CHAPTER THIRTY-ONE

The farther they drove away from the luxurious cabin the more Candice thought she could breathe, but she'd been wrong. Instead, anxiety gripped her with every stretch of mile. She'd left deception behind her, but ahead of her she faced a decision she dreaded.

Jarell pulled the car into a rest stop in Pennsylvania and parked next to a white SUV loaded with bottled water and rolls of toilet paper. Candice wondered whether they were heading somewhere or fleeing.

"Tell me what's wrong," Jarell said.

Candice looked away from the SUV. "Wrong?"

"You've been strangely quiet most of the trip." He took her hand. "And don't tell me you're staying quiet because you're afraid I'll fall asleep. We've gotten past that."

She bit her lip and pulled her hand away. "I can't see you anymore."

He laughed. "Very funny."

"I'm not joking."

His smile fell. "What are you talking about?"

She rubbed her hands together. "Somehow Dev found out the truth about me and he threatened to tell Fletcher. He wants five percent to stay quiet, but if I disappear he'd have no leverage over you. You can feign innocence."

His face changed. "What are you talking about?"

"Everything will be fine if you just follow what I say."

"You spoke to Dev?"

"Yes."

"Alone?"

"Yes."

"When?"

"When you were in the city."

"Why didn't you tell me this before?"

She hesitated. "Because—it doesn't matter."

"Of course it matters!"

"We can make this work as long as you do as I say."

"He wants five percent?"

She nodded.

His voice deepened. "Is that all he asked for?"

She knew better than to hesitate. She said the word swiftly, decidedly. "Yes."

His keen gaze sharpened. "Really?"

"I'm taking responsibility. This mess is all my fault. You were right, if I'd pretended to be your girlfriend we wouldn't be in this trouble."

Jarell sat back and leaned against the headrest. "I'll have to turn them down."

"You can't. You need this money. Not just you but your family and the employees who depend on you."

He straightened. "So you've made the decision for me."

"It's the best option. I have tried to think of other strategies but nothing works without sacrifice."

"And that sacrifice has to be us?"

"I'm sorry."

He rested his forehead on the steering wheel and swore. "I told you to come to me when you're in trouble, didn't I? Didn't I tell you to trust me?"

"I do. But this is bigger than us."

"You really think I can work with a man like that?"

"You have to."

"No, I don't."

"Think of your mother. Your brother. Your brother's family."

Jarell shot her a dark look. "You don't have to remind me about that."

"I'm really sorry."

"Stop saying that." He stepped out of the car.

Candice did the same and stared at him over the hood. "I mean it." It startled to drizzle, as faint as a mist, which struck her as odd since the sky was still blue with few clouds. Soft droplets fell on them as if the clouds didn't want to make the effort of getting them completely soaked but rather vaguely damp. "We can talk in the car."

Jarell shut his eyes, lifted his face to the sky. The rain silently wetting his face, causing it to shine. When he spoke she heard the pain in his voice. "I've already had to give up so much. And finally I've found something for me and you're telling me to give it up too."

"If you think—"

He ran a hand down his face before he looked at her. "I don't want to think. I don't want to think about how this is like a game. But if—if it were a game. If we were in FFP this wouldn't have happened. Do you know why? Because we always acted as if we were a team. You didn't go off on your own, we fought together. In the real world you act as if you're alone."

Candice glanced around the parking lot pleased people were too busy coming and going to pay attention to them. "Look, get in the car and I'll explain."

"Why should I get in the car?" Jarell rested his large forearms on the hood. "Am I an embarrassment to you? Are you ashamed to be seen with me?" He raised his eyebrows in a mocking display of surprise. "Maybe we shouldn't see each other anymore. That would solve everything."

She shook her head. "This isn't a joke."

He took a step back and let his arms fall to his sides. "Which is why I'm not laughing."

"I didn't come to this decision on my own. I *was* thinking about you."

"Really? You were thinking about me when you met with Dev behind my back? When you pretended to be happy for me the other day? How long did you practice telling me I couldn't see you again? That you had to disappear?"

"This is not what I wanted," she said, miserable.

"When will you realize that your actions have unintended consequences?"

"I said I was sorry. I just said—"

"You gave me no choice. You didn't consult me about any of this. You didn't give me a chance to share my opinions. Like a warrior leader you gave me orders and now you expect me to obey."

"That's not it."

"Then explain it to me. Why didn't you come to me? Why didn't you give—"

"Because I knew what you'd say," she cut in desperate

for him to understand, "and I didn't want—" She stopped. She couldn't finish the sentence without feeling ashamed.

"You didn't want to hear it," he finished for her. His tone no longer held pain, just weary resignation. "That's fine, you're not the first person who doesn't care what I have to say. Congratulations, you made my mother very happy. Her idiot son made her proud."

"Jarell, please, I didn't mean it like that."

He opened the backseat. "You drive. Wake me up when you're home."

CHAPTER THIRTY-TWO

She'd planned on never seeing Jarell again after New York. But that was before she'd fallen in love with him.

She never planned on missing him and feeling so wretched about it. He had every right to be angry with her. Staying away, having him freeze her out, felt like the right punishment. But she'd done the right thing. In time he'd see that.

'Darius' had left before saying goodbye to Edgar but as Darius, Candice created an email address and had sent him the pictures she'd promised him, plus a listing of other companies that could help him with web design. When Edgar eventually thanked her and opened the door to continue their friendship, she'd lied about being swamped with work and an upcoming business trip, but as much as she despised it, she'd gotten good at lying. If it protected him, then it was worth it. He deserved better. Plus, as Fletcher's nephew, he could never find out the truth.

At night, she tried a new game, not ready to return to the

world of FFP and memories of V. Unfortunately, it turned out to be a conventional save-the-world adventure set in the distant future that felt as imaginative as vanilla pudding—comforting but you knew what you were going to get—with actors who seemed more concerned with keeping their accents than getting into character, which left her feeling hollow instead of providing the escape she craved. No amount of puzzle rooms to probe, trials to experience and people to rescue seemed to fulfill her.

With reluctance she returned to FFP and every night she played with a ferocity she'd never had before. She talked to her cousin, took little notice of her roommates and worked.

And then, for the first time in years, she thought about another loss that had wounded her.

Candice remembered when she was just starting out as a video editor, when she used to bid on different projects. There was another person who started out as a rival then became a friend. He would tease and criticize her work. Because she started so young and she'd grown up in an environment where 'self-esteem' was the watch word, few would give their honest opinion. When she attended school the teachers would just nod and be impressed, when her mother home schooled her she and other instructors would do the same. No one felt the need to criticize her—being parentally praised was almost as bad as being a wall. Indulgent and protective words made her feel invisible. Unimportant. How could she improve if no one was willing to tell her where she needed improvement? She felt as if no one cared enough to see her get better.

However, she succeeded quickly and did her best to find her own weak spots and improve on them and felt she had only minor ones.

Until she crossed paths with him.

At first he was just Cut2Chase which she thought was a silly handle, but he wasn't silly at all. He was sharp. He teased her good naturedly, he called out her mistakes. It was unsettling at first. No one had been so forward with her. For most of her life, the ruling belief was either 'black girls are fearless and strong and natural leaders, so they didn't need to train, they were just genetically gifted' or 'black girls need extra protection due to their fragile egos and centuries of dispiriting treatment, so don't criticize or they'll strike out or be demoralized.'

Cut2Chase didn't seem to think either. He treated her like an equal. He made her fight and defend her decisions. He was intellectually stimulating.

At first, she'd been insulted and then challenged. Here was someone pushing her, driving her to be better, to be different. She credited him with giving her the skills she now possessed that made it easy for her to choose clients instead of having them choose her. Aside from Randall he became someone else's opinion she could trust.

In turn he trusted her. She learned that he was three years older (she later discovered that was a lie and he was actually two years younger than her, having used his father's information to set up an account since he was under age). That really shocked her that at fourteen he could be so sharp. By twenty he stunned her with his creativity.

She still remembered the text when he first offered her a contract. She'd thought he was joking.

C2C: *I've started a studio.*

Candice: *You can't afford me.*

C2C: *Try.*

Candice: *The price will astound you.*

C2C: *I'm waiting. Remember I know your basic rates.*
Candice: *But this will be different.*
C2C: *Go ahead.*
Candice: *You'll have to agree when I tell you.*
C2C: *Show me first.*
Candice: *$0*
C2C: *Try again.*
Candice: *Fine, then pay me what you think I'm worth.*
C2C: *I can't afford that yet.*
Candice: *Ha ha.*
C2C: *I mean it. But one day I will.*

He eventually gave her a roundabout number and they agreed on the project.

It had been the beginning of working together.

She remembered they both moved on from scrambling for freelance work. He eventually started a studio and hired her for different projects over the years. Still terse but kind. He and Randall made life bright.

But then Randall died and she'd felt too drained to reply to his messages. She'd also felt a little guilty by how much C2C reminded her of how life used to be. She'd wanted to distance herself from her past and who she'd used to be. She spent the next several years trying to be someone she wasn't. Buying a townhouse, dating guys she shouldn't have.

After emerging through her pain and realizing she was best alone she thought of him again and decided to reach out to him. When she emailed him, the message was never read and when she looked up his company website she saw that he'd sold it. She looked at the portfolio of projects and saw they were interesting and safe. Nothing stellar. Nothing that reminded her of him. The projects weren't close to the crazy interesting ones she'd known him for. She was sad she'd lost touch. She hadn't tried harder after Randall's death. She hadn't been a good friend. He was better off without her. But she did regret that she'd never gotten a chance to tell him how much he'd meant to her. It was no different now. Jarell would never know the truth.

She knew the pain would never leave but she'd grow used to it as she always had. She was better off alone. Caring hurt too much.

"THANKS FOR THIS," Alana said as Candice closed the trunk of her SUV after caring for a lovely Persian cat and its lecherous owner.

Candice wiped her forehead, the sticky summer sun plastering her clothes to her skin with sweat. "No problem."

Alana scrolled through her cell phone and reviewed her weekly schedule. "That's it for today. Oh...wait there's Alfonso. Can't forget about that." She made a note then sighed and put her cell phone away. "Shame about his former owner."

Candice stared at her alarmed. "Former? What do you mean?"

"He's in a coma."

"What?"

"Yes, distracted driving I think...or maybe he fell asleep at the wheel..."

Candice couldn't hear the rest. In spite of the blazing sun the parking lot became silent and dark. As if she'd been consumed by a dark mist. She felt the icy cold breath of fear cascading over her skin, causing her to shiver. Her greatest fear had come true. That the tentacles of death that had hovered so close around him would one day grab him and pull him down leaving her feeling helpless. She'd worried about him. Feared for him and now...now... Jarell was in a coma? Had he fallen asleep at the wheel? Had his insomnia come back?

Candice grabbed her sister's arm before she could get inside the car. "What hospital?"

Alana frowned. "I don't know."

"How could you not know?"

"I didn't ask."

Right, her sister only cared about the animals. That made annoying sense. Even if Alana knew which hospital Jarell was in, that mother of his wouldn't allow her to see him.

"What happens next?"

Alana stared at her, startled for a moment, then said, "I offered to take Alfonso for a couple of days—"

"I'll do it."

"But—"

"I said I'll do it. Don't argue with me." It was all her fault that Alfonso was alone. She'd eventually adopt him and take care of him. "What time did you plan to pick him up?"

"Candice, you're scaring me again. What is going on?"

"Just tell me the time!" She didn't care that she frightened her. She didn't care what her sister thought of her. She didn't care about anything except getting to the one thing that connected her to him. Even if it was just a cat.

"Tonight around seven but you really don't have to— Where are you going?" Alana asked when Candice turned.

"I have to run a few errands."

"I'm free the rest of the day. I can take you."

"No, that's okay. I'll get a ride home," she said then ran.

She ran not knowing exactly where she was going. She just knew she had to get away from her sister before she started to cry. Inside she screamed.

Jarell wasn't supposed to get hurt. Her plan was perfect. He was supposed to be okay. She'd endured three months without him, telling herself that he was fine. That she was fine. But this news forced her to realize it had all been a lie. She hadn't been okay. She'd been miserable. She'd been miserable for so long she hadn't recognized it. She hadn't realized how numb she'd become until she'd heard Alana's words: He's in a coma.

She remembered the cold way they'd parted. The hurt in his voice when he said goodbye. She'd been wrong to let him go. To not have tried to fight for him. He was right, she hadn't acted as a team; she'd pushed him away because she'd been scared of losing him. Now she might lose him forever without a chance to tell him how she really felt. Jarell had entered her life and brought brightness back in. She'd given credit to the game, but the truth was he'd been a big part of it. He'd made her believe she could belong in the world.

Nearly an hour later Candice entered her townhouse sweaty and exhausted. She took a shower. She had four hours before she had to pick Alfonso up. She didn't feel like eating, she didn't want to talk to anyone. She ignored her sister's calls and texts.

It was only when she looked in the full length mirror that she realized she'd put on the same clothes she'd worn to Randall's funeral—black slacks, a white shirt, but this time she'd added a black velvet tie. She ran her hand down the luxurious fabric remembering the moment Jarell had given it to her. Now he'd never see her wearing it. But she could honor him this way.

Her eyes remained dry as if her sorrow reached a pit too deep for tears. Maybe tears would come later, maybe they'd never come at all.

Regrets seized her instead of sorrow. Regrets that she hadn't done more. That the last words she'd said to him...

Candice looked at Randall's smiling picture. "Am I being crazy? I know this won't change anything. But it's something I feel I have to do. Even if I got a chance to see him, I'm not sure I would go and see him." She didn't want to see him in a hospital bed, attached to tubes keeping him alive. She wanted to remember him as he was. But was that being cowardly?

"I'm a coward," she said aloud, amazed by how the statement both shamed and freed her. She was forced to face her true self. Candice was a coward. That's why she hid. Adian and Darius and any other character she'd played had been the opposite of her true self. She'd been a coward all her life. Hiding her true self so she wouldn't get hurt and in turn hurt others. She thought of Alana's worried face, Jarell's pained eyes, Fletcher's admiration, Edgar's trust.

You don't know how you affect people. Jarell had once told her that. But that wasn't completely true. A small part of her had, a part of her didn't care. The part that guarded herself from the world.

But she cared now. She would let her armor fall and no longer live life as a constant battle and think of people as either allies or enemies to be used.

She stared at her reflection. Today she would stop being a coward. Today she'd face life as herself—fully, completely, no matter what happened.

It didn't matter if Candice was boring.

She could also be brave.

"*Darius?* You look so different without your glasses. You have such pretty eyes."

It took Candice a moment to process what she should say. She hadn't expected Sara to open the door. She briefly wondered if she and Jarell had gotten back together before the accident. She also looked surprisingly composed for such a stressful time. Candice cleared her throat wondering if she should continue the ruse a little longer. Probably best not to confuse the situation. She'd just take Alfonso and leave.

"Uh, thanks."

"I know you're surprised to see me. I swear, sometimes I think I see him now more than I did before we broke up."

Candice cleared her throat. "W-why did you?"

Sara sighed. "Crazy stress, the insomnia but then he told me he wasn't being fair to me because he'd met someone else while playing some game. Flames of Powder or something."

Candice's heart began to race. "Flowers of Fortune and Power?"

"Yes, that's it." She rolled her eyes. "As if I believed him.

I mean who gets dumped for a game, right? Then again some of those avatars just fulfill male fantasy, so how can a mortal woman compete? But enough about that, you're here for a reason, right?"

"I've come here for Alfonso. Alana should have called."

"I'm not sure about this. Poor Alfonso won't like it."

"I'll take good care of him."

"She's early," a deep voice said. Then a ghost from the past came into the room.

Candice backed away and hit the wall with a bang. She stared at Jarell. "You're here."

He frowned at her. "Why wouldn't I be here?"

"You're supposed to be in a coma."

"Why would I be in a coma?"

"Aaand that's my cue to leave," Sara said, swiftly grabbing her coat and purse. "Don't mess this up, I'm not looking after your cat." She motioned Jarell forward and he bent down so she could give him a quick peck on the cheek before she dashed out the door.

Candice studied the closed door wondering if she should follow. Maybe if she ran really fast...

"What are you doing here?" Jarell said.

"I thought you'd been in an accident. Alana told me you were in a coma."

Jarell folded his arms. "Why would she say that?"

"I don't know. I was supposed to pick Alfonso up because his former owner..." Candice hung her head. "Oh God could she have been talking about another Alfonso? Did I get it all wrong?"

"Alfonso's original owner is in a coma. In an accident that left Alfonso with one eye. The family put him up for adoption. I immediately liked him. I thought we'd get along great—he has one eye and I have one kidney." When she didn't respond to his attempt at humor Jarell said, "Anyway, I asked your sister to take him to a cat hotel because I'm going to be gone for a couple days."

"Oh." She felt like a fool. Alfonso came to greet her, rubbing his head against her leg. She crouched down and stroked him. "Sorry I made fun of his name."

"It's okay. I'm fine. You don't have to worry about me anymore." He turned.

Be brave. Be brave. Candice rose to her feet and said, "How's the business?"

Jarell released a tired sigh. "Just go, Candice."

"I'm sorry. I was wrong. At the time letting you go felt easier—safer—than losing you. I didn't tell you because I didn't want to hear you make a choice, I made the choice for you. I wasn't in control when my cousin got sick, many things in life I can't control, so when I have a chance I seize it."

He sat on the couch. "I lost the funding."

She stared down at him. "What? How?"

"I turned it down."

"Because of me?"

"Partly." He tapped his chest. "But also because of me. I didn't like how scared and desperate I'd become. I realized I couldn't be a true leader feeling like that. I still wasn't making good decisions no matter how much sleep I got. I realized I needed to take a step back. My mother isn't talking to me right now. But when I looked at the status of things again and talked with my Dad I saw that we're not in as much trouble as I'd first thought."

Candice cautiously sat down. "But the money. You still need it."

"And there are other ways. Other options. I learned that from someone. Signing that contract meant I had to give up a lot more than I was willing to. Part of it was myself. So as I've said you don't have to worry about me."

"If you need money I could sell my townhouse."

"You don't need to do that." Jarell stood. "Let me get his carrier."

"Or let me talk to Fletcher. Maybe—"

"No." He headed for his coat closet.

"I can stay and catsit for you then Alfonso wouldn't have to leave."

He opened it. "Why would you do that?"

She stood. "Because I want to help."

"What if I don't want your help anymore?"

"But you need—"

He slammed the door closed. "I don't need anything!"

"But you asked my sister for help."

"I asked your sister for a favor because I respect her. That's all. If she hadn't been able to do it I had other options. I'm not desperate, Candice. I don't need to be rescued. That's the problem with us. You come sweeping into my life anytime you think I need to be rescued."

"That's not true."

"Then why are you here?"

"Because I thought you were in a coma!"

"Exactly, you wouldn't have come otherwise. Am I wrong?"

She didn't have an answer. He was right. She only felt brave when she felt she had a reason and a purpose. Having a purpose didn't make her feel vulnerable. People didn't reject you when they needed you.

"Okay, you're right." She paused. "I have a confession to

make. It's something I've never told anyone." She took a deep breath. "I told my family I bought a townhouse for an investment and got roommates for extra income. But that's not the true reason. One night, a couple months after Randall had passed, I was watching reruns of this old TV show called "The Golden Girls" and I loved their friendship and I thought that if I bought a place and put an ad out like Blanche did I'd find a way to make friends too.

"It didn't work out that way. Being me wasn't enough. I wasn't interesting. I learned that people only notice me when I'm useful to them. When I'm not, I become invisible again. Except with you I felt the most myself. There are so many times you remind me of someone I used to know. I know that sounds cliché but it's true. But we lost touch, which was my fault and I tried to find him but he disappeared from my life and I am so tired of losing people I care about."

Jarell sighed. "Want something to drink?"

Candice flexed her fingers relieved he wasn't throwing her out. That was a good sign.

"I'll have one of your teas."

He made a face. "Come on then."

In the kitchen he pulled out the tea canisters, took out a mug then pointed to the sink and said, "You can get steaming hot water from that tap." He pointed to the third tiny faucet.

"Nice," Candice said pouring the water over the tea bag, its strong woodsy aroma scenting the air. "Aren't you going to join me in a cup?"

He handed her the sugar bowl. "I'd rather cook a lemon rind and eat it."

Candice shook her head and clicked her tongue. "I'll remember that."

Jarell leaned against the counter, letting his gaze fall to the ground. "So who was this guy you lost touch with?"

"Have you forgiven me, yet?"

He met her eyes. "No, but I might if you tell me the story."

She took a tiny sip of her tea, added a little more sugar, took another sip, realized she'd made it too sweet and set the tea down. "Okay. Years ago I used to have this guy I interacted with online. He was brilliant and although he was younger than me he had an old soul. Before he actually told me his age I'd thought he was really old like thirty or something. To be fair I was sixteen at the time. He was into video editing like me, actually he was more on the production end, but he started off bidding on different projects just for the practice.

"Actually now that I think of it, the funny thing is I always called him Jay, but sometimes I'd tease him and call him Superman because his name was different. Talk about geek humor. He got the reference immediately and we'd talk about it and other names." She bit her lip. "His name was like...it's been so long." She snapped her fingers. "His name reminded me of Superman's father's name: Jor-El."

"I know," Jarell said in a soft voice, that soft intimate way that always got her attention. But this time it was different, this time it was more knowing and significant than before.

Her voice caught and she stared at him as pieces slowly began to fall into place. Jarell. *Her* Jarell. She'd never put it together. They were so different. The Jarell of the past was more carefree, less regimented. But so much had happened to him. That was why he'd felt so familiar all this time. When he's said he'd known her much longer he'd meant it. "I lost touch with him and when I looked him up again I discovered he'd sold his business."

He held her gaze. "What do you think happened to him?"

"I think he gave up a lot to be there for his family."

"Are you disappointed? He's not who he once was."

"He's even more than I could have imagined. He's exactly how I remember him. He has terrible taste in coffee, but he's still sharp as ever and one person I always look forward to talking to. But his last name wasn't Ventura."

"Hmm...it's possible his mother didn't want him soiling the family name so he had to come up with another one."

"Oh." That made sense.

His gaze fell to the countertop and he traced a circle with his forefinger. "I didn't know it was you at first. I just liked Adian and as time went on there were traits that reminded me of you. It wasn't until we started chatting that I made the connection. That's why I wanted to talk to you. I wanted to make sure. And then I heard your voice—"

"And feel asleep."

Jarell shook his head, chagrin touching his face. "I don't know why that happened, but it was like I could breathe again. I could relax, I could be me again. Feel like my old self. It was overwhelming."

"So basically I made you pass out."

He frowned at her. "Stop focusing on that."

She shrugged. "I can't help it. It brought us together."

He nodded, lowered his gaze and drew another circle. "You're right."

"Wait, so all this time you knew who I was?"

"Yes."

"When were you going to tell me?"

"I honestly wasn't sure I wanted to. I used to have grand plans. I didn't want you to see me like this. Like a regular CEO of a boring company with familial responsibilities. Life didn't go as I'd hoped."

"Me neither. I didn't think I'd be stuck in a loop with everything and everyone changing around me. But the funny thing is I'm still me and you're still you. No matter what's changed, I still think you're amazing and interesting." She covered his hand, wanting him to look at her, prepared for him to pull away.

He didn't.

"You have no idea how much you affected me," he said in a husky whisper. "You made a smart-assed fourteen year old nerd feel like he mattered. I tended to scare off most people, not because I wanted to it was just how I was—brash, obnoxious, but you didn't care. And when I found out I couldn't scare you I knew I was in trouble. I didn't know what to do when your cousin died. You cut me out."

"I'm sorry."

"I know." He paused. "I think...I initially fell asleep because...I couldn't believe I'd found you again and...you felt safe. You calmed me. After that it was just...I liked being with you. I've had so few people in my life I can turn to, lean on, that's what you are to me. But more than that I want to be someone you turn to also. I want to be the person you can trust."

Candice squeezed his hand. "I do trust you. And I admit I do like rescuing you. But you also rescue me."

He took her hand and turned. "I want to show you something."

She held back. "Does this mean I'm forgiven?"

"Not yet."

She let him lead her to his bedroom and opened the door.

This time the sight of it didn't make her gasp or sad. The furniture they'd chosen together made Candice feel as if she'd come home.

"How's your insomnia?"

"Getting better." He turned to her. "But I have a new problem that keeps me up at night."

"What?"

He sat down on the bed and looked up at her. "I don't like sleeping alone."

She stepped between his legs and flashed a slow, sly grin. "Want me to buy you a teddy bear?"

"I want something money can't buy."

"Like?"

"Your trust."

She froze. "I just told you. I do trust you."

"Then tell me what really happened with Dev."

She released a shaky breath. "Why? It won't change anything."

His tone hardened. "It will change everything. Either tell me or go."

"It's not that I don't trust you. I just can't relive that moment again and I don't want to repeat what he said about you or about me. I won't because Dev has nothing to do with us. But if you think that means I can't be a part of your life I understand." She stepped away and turned, fighting tears.

"Fletcher guessed you'd say that."

She spun around. "Fletcher?"

Jarell nodded at her look of surprise. "Yes. I still talk to him."

"B-but you didn't get the funding."

A wolfish grin came and went. "No. But I did get another business opportunity. It wasn't easy but after a few more chats we came to an agreement. I told him the truth about you, we spoke about Dev. Fletcher had had his suspicions about him; the retreat was as much to reveal Dev's true character as a test for me. So what happened with you confirmed and exposed even more about Dev's tactics than Fletcher had expected. To say the least we weren't the first he'd tried to 'bargain' with. He told me they parted ways and then we spoke about you."

Candice waited, her heart racing. "And?"

"And he said that you loved me so much you'd never tell me what really happened with Dev no matter how much it hurt you because that's the kind of person you are. He told me to accept that."

She blinked back tears. "Can you?"

Jarell rose to his feet. "No."

Her heart fell.

"But I can practice." He unbuttoned the top of her shirt. "I want to practice long and often because I don't want to lose you again."

She started to shake. She didn't trust herself to speak.

He undid another button. "But I'll need your help. I guess you'll have to rescue me after all," he said with a note of irony.

Candice pushed him down on the bed with renewed courage, her heart rejoicing. "Good, because it's one of my favorite things to do." She stripped out of her clothes until all she had on was a pair of panties and the black velvet tie. "Hold on tight."

Jarell grabbed the tie and pulled her forward. "I don't plan to let you go." He kissed her then whispered against her lips, "You've permanently changed my mind about ties."

"I knew I would," she replied then kissed him back.

"And I'll hire a tailor to make us matching kaftans if you want."

"Really? I'd always wanted one. You'd do that for me?"

"Yes, in the colors of green, black and silver with a matching hat."

She laughed and threw her arms around his neck. Her heart buoyant. He'd get a traditional male garb made just for her in the colors of her favorite game. It would be their secret bond V and Adian walking side by side. He accepted her completely. "Thank you."

He chuckled pleased by her delight then held her gaze and whispered words in a different language. Words that transformed him into someone even more dear to her than he'd been moments before. Words spoken in Yoruba that held their own special magic.

The words 'I love you'.

He loved her. He loved her flaws, quirks and all.

"Very much," he added in English, holding her close before pressings his lips to hers.

And they didn't sleep at all that night.

As morning rose Candice watched the faint rays of sunlight peek through the blinds as she lay in his arms. She licked her lip before she said, "Want to go hiking someday?"

"Hmmm." She knew Jarell was half asleep and she wasn't sure he'd heard her question until he said, "How about this weekend?"

This weekend. She felt a fissure of panic. Unease. Was she ready? Someday was finally on the horizon. Soon someday would be today. She closed her eyes and sank deeper into his embrace. Soon the thought no longer frightened her. She could be happy again. She wanted to face the future with all its wild chaos. No more hiding. She could face life as herself with someone she loved and who loved her. She was ready to play a different game: One with higher stakes and greater rewards.

"Yes," she said with a smile, "this weekend sounds perfect."

ABOUT THE AUTHOR

Dara Girard, an award-winning, national bestselling author of more than fifty novels, from romance to suspense, loves telling stories.

Born in the US to immigrant parents, Dara enjoys pulling from her Jamaican, British, Nigerian heritage and exposure to various cultures to bring what reviewers and fans call "vivid emotional stories" to life. She is best known for her popular Henson Series, the mysterious Clifton Sisters, and the fun Black Stockings Society.

You can write her at:
contactdara@daragirard.com
or
P.O. Box 10345
Silver Spring, MD 20914
If you'd like to receive a reply, please send a self-addressed stamped envelope.

Visit her website to sign up for her newsletter and get sneak peeks, monthly updates on new releases, and special offers.

For more information visit
www.daragirard.com